Chapter 1

An ice-chilled breeze drifts past Ellen Carpenter, seated alone near her slightly opened living-room window. It eases past the same panes of glass her son Thomas had once gazed through, years ago, while eagerly awaiting her late-night arrivals from waitressing. With it being just the two of them for so many years, they clung to each other tightly for nearly everything.

Settling back into her couch, Ellen gazes at an old framed-photo of Tommy in his Little League uniform, hanging upon an adjacent wall. His goofy smile in that Giants uniform, with his hair all messy and a big wad of chewing gum stored-up in his cheek, reminds her of the fun loving boy in which she was blessed. It also allows her a slight reprieve from all of the sorrow.

She drifts back in time and remembers slowly tip-toeing into Tommy's bedroom, at three in the morning, just to sneak a glimpse of her baby boy sleeping. Oh, how watching Tommy snuggle that Red Power Rangers doll of his, how it would vault her heart to the top of Mount Everest in one easy bound. But now...that's all gone.

Sighing while gently stroking the barely visible wrinkles near the corner of her eyes, she laments of how those double-shifts at the diner seemed like two lifetimes ago.

Seems that Tommy was the only person in which Ellen had ever shared an unconditional love. Not one based upon her flawless beauty, or for her broad and steady shoulders to cry upon...it was just because she was his Mommy.

Thomas embodied everything she thought achievable in life. But now...that's all gone.

Ellen's long hair sags lifelessly in her view as she stares, nearly comatose, at her reflection in a nearby mirror. Her golden locks go unattended as the hour-eleven tolls from the grandfather clock that's been in her family for generations. But just like the proverbial tree falling alone in the forest, Ellen's broken-heart wasn't there to hear the clock's chiming, so sadly, it *does* go unheard.

Had it been an hour...a day...or the entire two months since Tommy's violent murder that she first sat here to contemplate a vacant future?

She does know one thing for certain...Tommy's unlimited expectations drifted away, like a fading deserts' mirage, that dreadful

Christmas Eve. Illusions so alluringly close, but never to drink from the well of her aspirations.

Ellen's warm smile and ever-inviting green eyes have been supplanted by the ghostly remnants of all those shattered dreams. Never to be spoken are the words, "Mom, meet your grandchild"...or Ellen's boastful pride in Tommy's impending graduation from Yale. That's all been replaced with the inherent devastation of burying your one and only child.

Walking over to the ajar living-room window, Ellen shivers, just realizing the room has nearly matched the February-in-New Jersey's frigid temperature. After sliding the window closed, she peers through the frosty glass and slowly fades into a long-past vision of her and Tommy, frolicking in the snow of their front yard...

...They're just completing Tommy's first-ever snowman. She chuckles noticing that he can't jump high enough to put the carrot in for a nose. After lifting him, Tommy aggressively jabs the orange stalk into the snowman's face, knocking Frosty's head clean-off. After leaping from her arms, they have a brief chase around the decapitated snowman. She catches him around the waist, they share an Eskimo-kiss then fall to the snow-packed ground, giggling all the way down...As their youthful

likenesses slowly fade away, Ellen turns from the window and cries,

"But now...that's all gone."

Chapter 2

Dreading another night of tormented dreams, Ellen stands wrapped in an old pink bathrobe in her kitchen. After scooping tomorrow's coffee into the machine's cradle, she realizes there's no filter to catch the grounds,

"Where's my head?"

After rubbing her ever-tired eyes, Ellen waves her hand in disgust,

"Screw it...I'll just get it in the morning."

She drags her pink fuzzy slippers across the floor, flips the fluorescent lights off then heads down the darkened hallway to her bedroom.

An hour or so later, her eye fluttering is evidence of a deep-sleep and hopefully a bit of solace for this anguished soul as she begins to dream...

...A twenty one year old Thomas is tearing into the gifts under their sparkling Christmas tree. He quickly opens a thin rectangular present, revealing the red power-tie hidden within,

"Wow Mom, this will be great for after graduation.

You know, for my first real interviews."

Reaching over their pile of gifts, he plants a kiss upon her forehead,

"You always know exactly what I need."

Ellen grins ear to ear in her accomplishment.

Her dream flashes forward to later that same evening as Thomas grabs for his winter jacket that's hanging near the front door. He slides his arms into the sleeves then engages the zipper as Ellen rushes up to him,

"Tommy... I don't need a Christmas present."

She tugs at his jacket,

"Just stay home and we'll go over your plans for the rest of your winter break."

Flamboyantly waving his arms in the air,

"I just won't have it Mom. Enough that they lost my luggage, but you go and buy me replacement clothes."

Shaking his head,

"Now, what would Santa say? And at least you need a new pair of fuzzy pink slippers."

Kissing him upon his cheek,

"Just be careful, the snow's really coming down."

Upon opening the front door he surveys the bleak wintery conditions,

"C'mon, I'm just walking a couple of blocks to Metro Drugs. I'll be fine little Miss Worry Wort."

He begins to whistle "White Christmas" then carefully makes his way down the icy stairs.

Ellen's dream takes an ominous turn as she violently clenches her pillow. The dream's scene changes to a black and white setting...

...The white tiled walls of a Morgue's Identification Room is the last place Ellen could have ever imagined she'd be spending her Christmas morning. She quivers and sways as the Coroner begins to pull back a small white curtain, obscuring someone lying upon an examination table.

A tall, dark skinned police detective attempts to steady Ellen's shoulders with his hand, but the sight of two gaping bullet holes riddling her baby's chest...its' just too much for her to bear. Detective Hayes catches Ellen as she crumples towards the floor.

The grainy video of the Metro Drugs' parking lot surveillance camera, it replays over and over in her dream as she jerks back and forth on the bed. Watching the police monitor, as the two shadowy figures in the distance stand over her Tommy, is now burned into her brain. But seeing those two flashes blaze from the muzzle of the taller figure's gun starts her screaming in horror.

...Now awake, panting and covered in sweat, she is rudely reminded that what started out as a beautiful memory of Tommy, was hiding her deepest guilt. Ellen let Tommy leave her house that terrible night, having closed the front door behind him for the very last time.

Chapter 3

The muffled sounds of incoming and outgoing air-traffic finds

Tommy's lost suitcases, sitting upon a gray steel shelf at Newark Airport,

with their EWR destination tags still attached to the handles. An airport

employee, Paul Samuels, enters the Claims Room front office and fumbles

with his keys,

"Bingo" Paul says aloud as he locates the correct key

from the bunch.

After unlocking the caged door, he walks to the back of the storage room.

Paul jostles a few adjacent bags and then comes across Thomas' black

luggage. He pulls a scanning gun off of his belt and runs the mechanism

across the destination tags,

"Finally, I've been looking for you two forever.

Where've you been hiding?"

Scooping up the bags, he then walks back to the cage's entrance just as a

woman wearing a blue blazer enters the room,

"So Paul, they've been here the whole time I see."

Paul looks at the floor,

"Sorry Ms. Whitfield, I would've sworn

they weren't here."

Ms. Whitfield shoots him an angry look,

"I'll just get them to their final destination.

Someone must be missing them, right Paul?"

He cowers while setting the bags at her feet,

"Yes Ms. Whitfield, I understand."

She misjudges their weight, drags them across the floor then sets them upon a dolly,

"You want something done right, just got

to do it yourself."

She hurriedly leaves the room and pushes the dolly down the hall. Once she's out of sight, Paul barks,

"You left the door open... you stupid bitch!"

Chapter 4

The mornings arrived and all's quiet but for the faint ticking of that old grandfather clock. The calm is broken when Ellen's front doorbell buzzes; although she doesn't move an inch to its beckoning. Seconds later the doorbell screeches again, forcing her to leave her isolation. She slowly makes her way to the front door, opens it then gently asks the dark-skinned man on her top-step,

"May I help you?"

He smiles,

"No, I'm here to help you ma'am. We at United Airways

want to apologize for delaying the retrieval of your lost

articles."

He unzips his jacket and pulls out an electronic tablet,

"If you could just sign this release form, I have

your luggage right here."

"My what?"

"The luggage we had lost on Thomas Carpenter's

flight 107 from Connecticut to Newark."

Ellen signs the invoice with a nervous hand,

"Where would you like me to put them ma'am?"

"Right here in the living room would be fine."

After tapping the snow off of his boots, he places Thomas' luggage down

with care as Ellen reaches for her handbag,

"Let me get you something…for being so nice."

"That's not necessary, just promise that you'll

have a blessed day."

She waves him goodbye, locks the front door then cautiously walks past

the suitcases.

After taking a seat upon her couch, Ellen gazes at the bags,

without a clue of her next move.

Chapter 5

By the third ring of her cell phone, Ellen's fixation upon Tommy's suitcases is broken and she notices it's been activated. She taps her Smartphone's screen and a voice from the phone asks,

"Ellen, is that you?"

"Yes, this is Ellen Carpenter. Who's calling?"

"It's Sophia Miller honey."

Ellen comes fully out of her daze,

"Sophia, oh my God...I didn't even look at the caller ID

It's so good to hear your voice honey. Sorry I haven't

called...I've been so distracted."

"No worries, I just miss you Ellen...how are you holding

up?"

Ellen searches for an honest answer,

"Good as can be expected...just seem to keep drifting in

and out."

Sophia's caring voice tells her,

"If and when you feel up to it, please stop by the office.

We all miss you so much."

"I will Sophia. Soon, I promise."

Ellen looks over at Tommy's suitcases,

> "I just have to put some...baggage away first."

> "That sounds like a great idea...Take care of your business and then when you're ready, come and see me."

> "I definitely will Sophia...sorry I haven't reached out much to you since Tommy's..."

Sophia interrupts,

> "Shhhhhhh, no apologies needed sweetie. I love you and whenever you need me...I'll be here."

Ellen brushes back the hair from her face,

> "I love you too Sophia."

She tightens her bottom lip and slaps herself on the knee,

> "I just need to take this damn bull by the horns... and get er' done."

Sophia hoots,

> "Now that's my girl...now go do your thing and I'll see you soon. Bye-bye love."

Ellen sets down the phone, walks over to the luggage and grabs their handles. She struggles with the weight, but manages to lift the bulk then carries them down the hall to Thomas' bedroom.

Chapter 6

The busy sounds of justice-in-action echoes through the District Attorney's office-complex. People are bustling through the maze of desks and hallways of the third-floor offices. In one such office, seated behind his large oak desk, District Attorney Scott Phillips flips through a file...looking for that elusive ah-ha moment. He tosses the folder on his desk then pushes the intercom's red button,

"Can you come in here for a second Sophia?"

Her voice squelches back,

"Certainly Scott, I'll be right there."

D.A. Phillips leans back into his leather chair and runs his fingers through his thick, slightly graying brown hair. He yawns and flexes his mammoth arms; the same arms that landed Scott a National All-American award for Offensive Lineman thirty years ago...the first Ivy-Leaguer to do so since the 1930's. Luckily for Scott, with his daily workout regime, he's been able to pretty-much keep the same physique since college. Sophia's petite-frame walks through his door; Scott shakes off his frown and scans her appearance...like a boy watching his mom getting ready for work,

"My, don't YOU look sharp this morning Mrs. Miller."

She quickly responds with a pirouette that gently twirls her Donna Karan skirt,

"Why thank you sonny-boy...very nice of you to notice."

As Sophia takes her seat across the desk, Scott picks-up the folder he's been working on,

"Would you please contact Detective Hayes for me?

I need to speak with him about the Carpenter case."

Sophia's eyebrows crown,

"The Carpenter case...You mean Ellen's son

Tommy, right?

Sophia reaches over and taps his hand,

> "Scott, I've worked for you over fifteen years now
>
> ...and know you like a book. You don't have to feel
>
> guilty honey."
>
> "Guilty? What the hell?"

She cuts him off in mid-sentence,

> "I've seen the sparkle you've taken towards Ellen
>
> over the years. Like when she was doing her paperwork
>
> and how you couldn't take your eyes off of her."
>
> "I didn't think anyone..."

Sophia cuts him off,

> "Remember, I'm the one you dictated that beautiful
>
> recommendation letter for Thomas' admission to Yale."

Scott swivels his chair to the side and points to the Yale Law School
Diploma hanging upon his wall,

> "I just KNEW something positive would finally come
>
> from all that hard work of mine out in law school."

Sophia's voice carries a serious tone,

> "And it's been seven years since you lost your Sarah.
>
> I know that she'd want you to find someone nice Scott."

They take a second to contemplate her remarks then he lovingly replies,

"My Sarah...she really was a great girl."

"The best Scott...the absolute best."

They smile in remembrance then he humorously remarks,

"Okay mother-hen...I'll take your counsel under

advisement. But for now, can you please find

Detective Hayes and have him report to me as

soon as possible. He's been working with Ms.

Carpenter...I mean Ellen, on her son's case. Thanks."

"No problem sir, I'm on it."

Sophia sprints out of the office as Scott picks up a picture frame housing a

photo of him and Sarah. Stroking her image with his burly thumb, he then

places it back on his desk and gets back to his work at hand...Justice.

Chapter 7

Ellen stands motionless, intently scanning Thomas' bedroom. His Patrick Ewing poster and N.Y. Mets pennants still hang upon the walls.

A framed photo of Thomas' father, adorned in his army sergeant's uniform, sits upon the nightstand next to his bed. She lifts one of the suitcases and places it atop the comforter then replays her actions, placing the second next to the first. She walks over to Tommy's nightstand and picks up the photograph,

> "I just wish that you could have seen him
>
> grow-up Charles. Thomas would have made
>
> you so proud."

Ellen chokes back a tear,

> "How different it could have been. If only that
>
> sniper didn't find you so young my love."

After kissing Charles' image, she drifts back to the memory of her in the hospital delivery room...

> "Charley...I can't do this!" Ellen screams into her
>
> flip-phone that's being held by a nurse.

His voice calmingly emanates from the receiver,

> "Just do what the doctor says babe...breathe and push."

"Listen to your husband Ellen. One last push and we're

home" urges her OB/GYN.

Moments later Tommy's loud crying bursts Ellen into tears,

"We did it Charley...your son is here!"

"I hear him babe...our little screaming soldier...

loud and clear!"

...Ellen re-emerges from her beautiful recollection, but sadly then

also remembers the pain of losing her Charles just two weeks later in

Somalia. Hugging the photo close to her chest,

"That's the closest you ever got my dear...

just those first sounds of our Tommy."

Stiffening her bottom lip, she puts down the picture then tentatively

unzips the first suitcase...hands shaking as she tugs the metallic flange.

Opening the lid, she then stares at Tommy's neatly folded pants

and shirts...so many memories folded-up in these suitcases. Turning to

the closet and grabbing a group of hangers from the wooden cross-rod,

Ellen hangs shirt after shirt and pants just the same. She reaches into the

second suitcase, moves some clothes around and spots Thomas' ultra-soft

beige cashmere sweater...the one she had bought him on that wonderful

day in New York City. Raising the sweater to her face and taking in a deep breath, she desperately searches for Tommy's faded scent. As she drifts

off into thought, she silently lips the word,

"Tommy."

...The rhythmic beating of train track against wheel churns as Thomas and

Ellen sit side-by-side. They're playfully nudging each other during their

short New Jersey Transit trip into Manhattan.

"Last stop Penn Station. All departures and

connections from Penn Station" blares from

the public address speakers.

The train suddenly comes to a halt then moments later, the doors slide

open. The other passengers depart and speed away as Ellen and Thomas

trail at a much slower pace. They exit the platform elevator, walk into

Penn Station and weave a trail across the busy station's floor.

"After you my dear" Thomas gallantly says while

Ushering her onto the escalator.

As they near the end of their lift up to street level Ellen turns to him,

"This is my favorite part Tommy."

"What's that Mom?"

She takes-in an animated breath, then exhales with her familiar

flamboyance,

"That surging wave of current running through

your chest…when you first hit New York City's

energy."

They reach the top of the escalator then emerge onto 34th Street,

"So, where are we off to Mom?"

She says back with a smile,

"We've got ALMOST everything for your first

semester away."

"Oh c'mon now mom…you've done enough

already."

"Well…you did all the hard work Tommy. That

beautiful brain of yours got the full academic

scholarship to Yale."

With pride, she raises her clutched hands to her chest,

"My sonny boy…Going to Yale…and with all those

Richie Riches up in Connecticut, you'll need something

special for those bigwig parties you'll be attending."

She points her finger down the street,

"The store is up on Forty-Fifth Street…so let's kick-up

our heels mister."

Thomas lightheartedly bumps his shoulder into hers then they head down the street.

...Ellen comes back to reality while folding that memorable sweater. She walks over, places it upon a shelf in his closet then makes the short trip back to the suitcases. After completing her task, Ellen slides the now lightened suitcases off the bed and one accidentally falls to the floor on its side. A wallet-size photograph pops out of the suitcase front pocket, coming to a rest at her feet.

Picking up the snapshot, she then takes a seat on the edge of Tommy's bed as every hair on her body stands at attention. Ellen raises the image up to eye-level and a lovely young couple, arm-in-arm, comes into her view,

"Who's that girl with my Tommy? My God...

she's lovely."

She notices the girls long blond hair and fair skin,

"Kinda resembles...me."

Ellen turns the image over and in Tommy's familiar script is written,

Tommy/Chelsea + Spud

"Chelsea, huh?"

She flips the picture over and studies it,

"Oh...that must be Spud" after noticing a small

dog in the picture's background.

She lays back, places her head upon Tommy's pillow and holds her

wonderful surprise near,

"This is just like you Thomas....baffling me with

your riddles and surprises ever since you could talk."

Chapter 8

Sophia, sitting at her desk and in mid-assignment, hasn't noticed Detective Hayes' tall, dark and handsome frame patiently waiting for her attention,

"Uh-hmm" Derrick coughs, vying for her

notice.

Sophia's looks up from her computer, spots Derrick standing in front of

her desk then flips her hair,

"Well...hello there Detective Perfect, right down to

his Armani suit and Georgio Brutini dress shoes.

How may I be of assistance to YOU today?"

He flashes Sophia a roguish grin while stroking his manicured Van Dyke,

"I'm here to see the Big Guy...Is Scott available?"

Sophia continues scanning her eye-candy,

"For you honey...the world. Let's just check first."

She pushes the intercom button,

"Excuse me sir, Detective Hayes is here to see you.

Do you have a free minute?"

Scott's voice comes over the speaker,

"Sure Sophia, send him right in."

Derrick straightens his tie, winks at her and dips his head to acknowledge her assistance. He heads towards the D.A.'s office as she watches his backside saunter away,

"Yummy...If I were only thirty years younger."

She laughs at herself then gets back to work at her computer.

Derrick leans partway through the half-open D.A.'s door. Scott's on the phone, but waves him in and points to the chair in front of his desk. Derrick takes the seat and patiently waits for his turn as Scott barks into the phone,

"Listen, I'm getting serious pressure from the Governor,

so just make it happen. On my desk...no later than three

o'clock...TODAY!"

He slams the phone down,

"Sorry about that Derrick...just juggling ten things

right now."

Derrick waves in an understanding manner,

"No problem...by the way, I've got some information

on the Carpenter case. Well, not directly related to it

yet, but I've got a hunch."

"Okay, I'm game. We've hit a stone wall with that

investigation...what's your hunch?"

Derrick reaches into his suit jacket's pocket, pulls out a small notepad

then flips through a few pages,

> "I've done some new homework. For two months
>
> now I've struggled with this one Scott. No damn
>
> evidence...no fucking sense to it."

Remembering back to catching Ellen from falling to the ground after

viewing her son's body,

> "I just gotta get this done Mr. District Attorney."

Derrick raps his fist upon Scott's desk. Quickly smiling, he then grabs a

pencil and taps it to his temple.

> "So I did some digging. Turns out there were four
>
> other murders on Christmas Eve, in a twenty mile
>
> radius, that I believe are all related."

Scott's eyebrows rise,

> "Related...how?"
>
> "The first two were Sylvia and Max Weinstein,
>
> during a home invasion in Springfield."

Derrick rechecks his notes,

> "Next was Thomas Carpenter in the parking

lot of Metro Drugs...in Union."

"Where are you going with this Derrick?

Their indoor surveillance video was useless."

Derrick gestures with his hand for Scott to wait,

"Just bear with me...the fourth was a random

shooting in Elizabeth on Broad Street. Then, last

but not least, the hit-and-run of a homeless

"John Doe" near the on-ramp to the Goethals Bridge.

Derrick flips to another page in his notebook as Scott interjects,

"And these deaths are related how?"

He spins the notebook around for Scott to survey,

"Look at the map I drew... it follows the timeline of

each of the murders. I did it on Google Maps too

and it fits perfectly."

Derrick points at the map,

"It all starts in Springfield with the Weinstein

murders. Their house is just two blocks in from

Morris Avenue."

He traces the map's route,

"I think these scumbags continue down Morris

Avenue, stop at Metro's and pistol-whip the clerk

before robbing the store."

Derrick forcefully taps the pencil on the notepad,

"That still bites my ass."

"What's that Detective?"

"How a business like Metro's will definitely

have an operational exterior camera for some

parking-lot dispute with a neighboring business...

but they don't give a shit enough to make sure

their inside surveillance is working properly."

Derrick composes himself then continues to follow the map with the

pencil,

"They waste Thomas Carpenter in Metro's

parking lot then keep heading east on Morris,

turn left on Broad Street and come upon Sally

Tithes...and for no good reason, shoot her right in

the face...while she was on her way home from

shopping and with a handful of fucking Christmas

presents."

Scott sinks into the back of his chair as the detective continues with his rationale,

"A few minutes later, they're getting back on I-278 and run over this homeless guy and leave him to bleed-out in the snowstorm. In my opinion, they're heading back to their home-base ...Staten Island."

He slaps the notebook with his hand,

"It all works...time-wise. I've made the trip myself and it fits right down to the minute. Only problem was the snowstorm knocked out all the cameras on the bridge that night. There are no records for the timeline that I've nailed it down to."

Scott scratches his chin,

"Tell me what I can do to help you Derrick. We've worked our magic before buddy and I'm always rewarded by trusting your instincts."

"Just get those different towns to share their info with me. Comparing shell casings, slugs and whatever other evidence they may have obtained...

maybe I can tie-up all these loose ends."

"Consider it already done Detective. You'll have the

full support of the D.A's office at your fingertips."

Derrick stands and shakes Scott's hand,

"We're going to nail these sons of bitches Scott.

I can feel it in my gut."

"Well, go do your detective thing...I'll do my D.A.

thing. I'm on it."

Derrick beats his fist to his chest then leaves the office. Scott picks up the

phone and begins making the appropriate calls to fill the Detective's

requests.

Chapter 9

Sitting alone in her kitchen just before daybreak, Ellen's
pondering her mired ways when Sophia's request to visit the D.A's office
comes to her mind,

> "You know…Sophia's right…I just need to stand up
> and fight for Tommy. He'd be so disappointed if he
> saw me wallowing in all of this self-pity."

Looking at his baby-pictures hanging on the wall,

> "I taught him to never, not EVER let anything stand
> in his way."

Rising from her chair, she lifts her chin high as her sorrowful expression is
supplanted by one of determination,

> "I'm going into work...no ifs ands or butts."

Clapping her hands together she then heads to her bedroom to get ready
for her trek.

Ellen pulls her blue convertible into the D.A.'s office underground
parking garage then guides her Mustang into the first available parking
space.

> Is she ready for this morning, or has she come
> back to soon?

Looking at the laminated photo of Thomas and Chelsea that now hangs from her keychain,

"Thank you Tommy for giving me the strength..."

After taking a deep breath and with resolve,

"...to go on."

The elevator doors of the third floor slide open and the morning shift of people pour out. Ellen stands in the back of the elevator and is last to exit,

"I'll just sneak in...go see Sophia...say my hello's

and tell everyone that I'm doing fine.

She walks down the hall and over to a large frosted-glass door. She pulls on the ornate gold handle, strides into the D.A's office and scans the space. The typist's are typing and the filers are filing as she walks slowly through the room, hoping a friendly face takes notice. Her heavy load is finally lifted as from across the busy floor, Sophia catches sight of her and calls out,

"Now there's my girl!"

Sophia waves Ellen over, then scrambles from behind her desk to meet her halfway. The dear-friends share an embrace then Sophia lightly grasps Ellen's wrists,

"I wish you would have told me..."

Ellen cuts her off in mid-sentence,

"I wanted to go low-key."

Ellen lightly grasps back,

"It's just so good to see you Sophia."

Sophia places her free hand on Ellen's shoulder,

"I couldn't agree more. But at least I could've

scheduled a lighter morning...we need to catch

up. How about sharing my lunch break with me?"

"That sounds great...and I've got some big news."

"Ooooo...big news. You know how I love the

juicy stuff."

"It's not really juicy Sophia...but I'm so excited

to sit down and tell you what I found."

As they turn and walk back to Sophia's desk, a few co-workers come over

to greet Ellen,

"Ellen...how are you doing?" calls out her friend Sarah.

"The office hasn't been the same without that

smile of yours" states a paralegal named Cindy.

"I'm doing much better girls. Actually, I'm thinking

of coming back to work...at least part-time."

Sophia chimes in with her reaction,

> "Are you sure you're ready for that?"

> "That's one of the things I wanted to

> talk to you about Sophia."

Sophia puts a hand on Ellen's shoulder,

> "12:30 sharp at the Mark Twain. There are

> a few things I need to tell you too...okay?"

Ellen looks at her with a puzzled expression,

> "What do you mean?"

> "12:30...okay sweetie? It's all fine, trust me.

> Now girls, let's get back to work."

From behind Sophia's desk, Scott peeks through his vertical blinds

shielding his office from the rest of the office-staff's space. He spots Ellen

talking with Sophia and nervously taps his foot,

> "What am I twelve years old?

Ellen turns towards him and his heart skips a beat, noticing that her eyes

easily out-shimmer the emerald pendant hanging around her neck,

> "Oh my..."

He scans the rest of her statuesque 5'9" figure, surveying how her black

dress perfectly complements her alabaster skin,

"Easy there, get a hold of yourself Scotty."

Ellen notices Scott's stolen glances out of the corner of her eye and is warmed by the attention. She playfully bites her bottom lip then runs her hands through her golden hair. Sophia claps her hands together, hurrying the girls back to work,

"Come back soon Ellen, we miss you" the girls

say in unison as they scurry away.

Ellen steps over and hugs Sophia,

"I'll meet you there...12:30 sharp."

Ellen releases their embrace, walks towards the office's front door and waves to a few other friends along the way. Sophia heads back to her desk and sees two slats on Scott's blinds suddenly closing,

"No Mr. District Attorney...you're not infatuated

much? Hmmm...I've gotta get those two kids

together somehow."

Sophia takes a seat as her matchmaking-brain shifts into overdrive.

Chapter 10

Derrick flips his wrist and checks the time on his Rolex...he's

waiting for Springfield's Chief of Police Welker to finish with his phone

call. Seated behind his desk, the Chief's large belly shakes as he bellows

into the phone's receiver,

> "Just do what I say Cucchinelli...it's your ass
>
> on the line!"

Chief Welker slams the receiver to its mount,

> "Sorry about all that" the Chief apologetically
>
> says as he turns to greet Derrick. "It's Detective
>
> Hayes, correct?

They share a handshake across the desk as the Chief says,

> "I watched all the news coverage about you solving
>
> the Ramsey triple murder last year, impressive
>
> work detective. How'd you get that asshole to
>
> confess?"
>
> "Grass roots detective-work and a bit of old-
>
> fashioned geology..."

Derrick takes his thumb and grinds it into his opposing palm, like a mortar

to pestle,

"...slow and steady pressure will always

win-out in the end Chief. Oh, and before I forget,

D.A. Phillips wanted me to send his thanks for all

of your assistance."

"Well anytime I can help the D.A's office and the

State Police, I consider it an honor."

The Chief grabs the Weinstein file from a pile on his desk, flips through its

contents then hands the file to Derrick,

"Take a gander at these pics detective...doesn't

look pretty. The Weinstein's daughter Alexis

found them three days after the shooting."

Derrick examines the crime scene photos as the Chief continues,

"We've got one motive, robbery... one broken

window as their main entry point and almost

no trace evidence. The only thing of value is

the slug we dug out of their hardwood floor...

and that's pretty much mangled."

"Not even one hair Chief?"

"Oh, we've got plenty of hairs Detective...they

had three dogs and four cats. After a few days

without feeding their pets...let's just say that the

crime scene was strongly compromised."

There's a knocking on the Chief's door then an attractive female officer

enters the office. Her eyes sparkle when she notices Derrick,

"Chief, I've got that ballistics report you asked for."

She hands him the folder then flirtatiously asks,

"Anything YOU need Detective? Coffee, tea...

full body search?"

Chief Welker quickly responds,

"That'll be all Officer Martin...thank you."

She winks at Derrick while leaving the office as the Chief surveys the file's

contents,

"It WAS a 38 Special."

He hands Derrick the file,

"I've had the results sent over to your crime lab.

They can check our slug's distorted striations

against any others you've collected."

He stands then salutes Chief Welker,

"Chief, thanks again for Springfield's help.

If there's anything I can do to reciprocate, just call."

Chapter 11

Seated at the Mark Twain Diner's back booth, Ellen stirs her coffee then raises the cup to take a sip. As the hot liquid takes the chill out of her body,

"Ah, like the sweet nectar of the gods."

She cradles the mug and notices Sophia entering the diner's front doors. Sophia spots Ellen as she removes her wintry coat then gestures to the hostess that she'll be joining her friend in the back. Ellen stands and hugs Sophia as she reaches the table,

"I can't tell you how good it is to see

you Sophia."

They take their seats on opposite sides of the booth as their waitress approaches,

"Hello dear" the waitress says to Sophia. "I'm

Sharon and I'll be your server today…coffee?"

Sophia nods her head then Sharon shuffles off. Ellen asks,

"So what's up?"

"You first…you've got some big news to spill?"

Ellen reaches into her purse,

"Look at this Sophia."

Ellen pulls out her keychain,

"Tommy had a girlfriend."

Sophia takes the keys and eyes the image,

"Oh my...she's gorgeous. Kinda looks like

you Ellen...who is she?"

"I know, that's what I said. Her name's Chelsea...

but that's all I got...you know Thomas and those

puzzles of his."

Sophia chuckles and shakes her head in agreement as Ellen continues,

"I'm assuming she goes to Yale, but I'd love to know

more about her. Maybe when I get back to work

we can use our resources to track her down."

"That's what I wanted to discuss with you Honey."

Ellen fidgets in her seat,

"What Sophia...is something wrong?"

Sophia touches Ellen's hand,

"It's not so much wrong...just a requirement for

your coming back to work."

"Okay...what's the D.A's mandate?"

Sophia quickly answers back,

"It's not Scott silly-girl...he's nuts about

you."

Sophia's eyes widen; hoping Ellen has missed her revelation of Scott's hidden feelings.

"He's what?"

Sophia nonchalantly waves her hand,

"I mean he loves the work you do."

Sophia reaches into her pocketbook, pulls out a group of papers and hands them to Ellen,

"New Jersey Law requires that anyone employed

by the D.A. must first undergo at least three group

sessions of supervised grief-management as a

condition of their return."

Ellen scans the paperwork,

"So, they want me to see this Dr. Alton before

I can go back?"

Just then, their waitress places Sophia's coffee in front of her,

"You ladies ready to order?"

Sophia opens her menu then points at her selection,

"The number 3, over-easy with rye toast."

Sharon scribbles down the order then looks for Ellen's response. Ellen

thinks for a moment,

"I'll have the same, but with an English

muffin."

Sharon writes it down, grabs the menus then leaves the table.

"Ellen, lunch is on me...and don't fret about

the doctor. It'll be good to share with others

who've been through the same experiences...

trust me doll, okay? And you can come back

to the office after your third session."

"Okay Sophia, you always know what's best...

whatever it takes."

They lift their coffee cups and toast to Ellen's future recovery.

Chapter 12

The deep-bass of an old-school rap song bellows out from a set of oversized stereo-speakers. The vibrations fill the dark, basement apartment of Haitian brothers Luc and Philippe Detaile'. They're playing each other a rousing game of video-soccer on their big-screen television. With elation, Luc jumps all of his 5'3" off the couch after his team scores the decisive overtime goal. He dances in front of his lighter-skinned, substantially larger brother Philippe...goading him with a victory lap around the room.

Their two African American counterparts, LeSean Jeffries and Quincy White, are trying to talk over Luc's outburst while sitting on a nearby couch. Quincy grabs a remote off his armrest, mutes the music then begins to roll a fat blunt. LeSean raises his muscle-bound arm and adamantly yells out,

"I'm telling ya Quincy...I just cut that fuckin'

bitch right off!"

Quincy stops rolling the joint, lightly taps on the top of his afro and glares at LeSean,

"Nigga'...you're full of some lyin' shit."

Without hesitation LeSean snaps back,

"If I'm lyin'...I'm mother fuckin' dyin'

you asshole."

Luc chimes-in,

"Go look in the freezer if you doubt

LeSean's good word Q-mon'...behind

the pizzas in a zip-lock baggie."

Quincy puts down his tray, darts from his seat and quickly reaches the

refrigerator. He opens the freezer door, pokes through the contents and

grabs the baggie. After shaking it, he spots a frozen finger still wearing a

large diamond ring,

"Now that's some hardcore shit LeSean.

When I heard that your cousin Renee was

setting you three boys up together...man,

I knew you were knockin' over an occasional

liquor store...but you boys are fuckin' crazy!"

Philippe adds in his two-cents,

"Crazy is as Crazy does Quincy...we're keeping

that old-lady's Ice on ice for a few months more...

then when the heat dies down, we can pawn our

yearlong haul down in Philly."

Luc prods LeSean on further,

>"LeSean, please tell our friend Q-mon why you shot that poor lady on the street that night in the snow."

LeSean raises his eyes and chortles with pride,

>"Cause I had one bullet left in the mother fuckin' chamber."

Luc high-fives LeSean as Phillippe continues,

>"That's one sick mother fucker right here Quincy. Twas' a nice bounty that snowy night for sure. Between that old couple's stuff and the liquor store's cash...we took in over ten large don't ya know. Not even counting the old bitches' ring. Cousin Renee's sure gonna be proud of us three."

LeSean taps his finger to his chin,

>"Renee's a damn badass Q...those two years in the joint with him...he taught me everything I know. Like always to be extra suspicious of those mother fuckers who are closest to you. Keep

your enemies close, and your friends even closer."

LeSean cracks his knuckles while noticeably glaring at Quincy,

"I was just thinking...that makes you the only other

LIVING person who knows exactly what we've

been up to this past year. Well that is YOU and

old Grannie upstairs...but she got a touch of the

dementia, so I doubt she's telling anyone anything."

An unsettled look overcomes Quincy...seems the gravity of his

companions crimes has finally come into 20/20 focus. He nervously

chortles as the three scowl at him, for what seems to be an eternity.

An alarm clock on a nearby shelf blares out and breaks the mounting
tension as Quincy shrieks,

"Ahhhhh".

The edgy moment quickly passes as the others begin to laugh. Quincy

takes a deep breath then defiantly yells,

"Y'all need to stop fuckin' with me...and turn

off that damn alarm."

Luc quiets the noise as Philippe says,

"Tis' Grannie's pill alarm Q-mon...

chillax brother."

Luc leans over from his seat then yells up the stairwell leading to

Grannie's upstairs apartment,

"Grannie...tis' 5:30...Take your pills Dearie!"

Quincy retakes his seat, grabs the remote and cranks back up the tunes.

Chapter 13

The inviting red suede sofa in Dr. Alton's Healing Room has comforted more than its share of pain. The perfectly matched crimson blanket draping the couch beckons out to those who have suffered the worst of atrocities...or so Mrs. Duvall thinks to herself as she dusts around its matching coffee table.

She adjusts her silver coif, rearranges a few magazines on the table and in a pseudo-man's voice says aloud,

"Mrs. D...We need the magazines to look

like they have that...care-free look...get it?

So brilliant...but he's such a nerd."

Dr. Alton's statuesque 6'3" enters from the kitchen of his spacious home/office and he greets his longtime assistant,

"Good morning Mrs. D...lovely to see you

this fine winter morn."

"Good morning Jeffery. Your weekly schedule

is on the desk...and so is your can of coke. How

can you drink that syrup so early in the morning

young man?"

He walks over and swigs a good portion of the can's contents,

"It's my Leche de Madre Mrs. D."

She's puzzled as he finishes the soda,

"It's my mother's milk."

He crushes the can, tosses it into the receptacle and walks over to the red

sofa. A look of accomplishment appears on his face as he adjusts its silky

blanket,

"We've done some blessed work here Mrs. D."

"Don't know about my role Jeffrey, but you

have aided in some incredible healing...hundreds

of stories over the past eleven years."

Dr. Alton stiffens his stature,

"Well all righty then...let's get this day

started, shall we my dear?"

He grabs his schedule off his desk then heads back to his kitchen. Mrs. D

returns to her cleaning tasks and lovingly states,

"What a wonderful nerd."

Chapter 14

The repetitive flip-flop of Derrick's windshield wipers come to an end as his Mercedes reaches the top of the Weinstein's driveway. The driver-side gull-wing door opens; Derrick exits the car and pushes the button on his designer umbrella's mahogany handle, unfurling a nearly tent size covering. He approaches the Weinstein's front door...for what must seem like the umpteenth time in the past week or so,

"There's just got to be something I'm

missing."

Pulling a lone key from his pocket, Derrick unlocks the door then ducks under some police crime tape. The still lingering odor of death instantly shifts him into Detective-mode. What appears on the surface to be a leisurely stroll through the Weinstein's many rooms is actually Derrick's way of putting himself into "the zone". These are tried-and-true methods that he's formulated since the academy...the same one's that sparked his promotion to Lead Detective by the time he was only twenty-eight,

"Writers write...pitchers pitch...Detectives...

they detect you asshole!"

He walks into the master bedroom and over to the taped outline of Sylvia Weinstein's body...the pooled blood from her dismembered finger is today's focal point. Derrick squats down and envisions Sylvia's torment at the hands of those damn animals. Lying down next to her outline, he mimics Sylvia's positioning on the floor when an investigative thought bursts to his mind,

"Wait a minute..."

Flashing through the original crime scene photos, Derrick recalls Sylvia's mostly unsoiled blouse and the blood stained pen that was left next to her body,

"Someone would normally hold a dramatic

wound like hers really close to their chest."

Derrick lifts his head from the floor and rescans Sylvia's outline,

"But her blood pooling is away from her chest...

she musta been trying to hide something very

important from them."

Smoothly rolling from his back to his knees, Derrick then reaches into his suit jacket and pulls out a small magnifying glass,

"I'm going old-school Sherlock Holmes on

ya here Sylvia."

He intently views the blood pool and notices that there's something wedged in hardwood floor slats. Pulling out his cell phone, he then taps its screen and a voice quickly answers,

"Derrick...what's up my brother?"

"Paulie...has the Weinstein house been fully processed? I need to grab something... don't know what it is yet...but it's definitely something."

"Give me a second buddy...I'll check."

Moments later, Derrick's broad grin indicates a positive outcome to his question,

"Man, that's great to hear...you just made my day buddy-boy."

Derrick hangs-up, pulls out a small men's grooming kit from inside his suit jacket and unzips the little black case. After removing a small pair of tweezers from the kit, he kneels down and gets right next to the blood stain, studying it from every angle.

He takes the tweezers, probes the sanguine-runoff then finally his eureka moment has arrived...a small strip of blood-soaked paper is wedged between a crack in the floor. He carefully grips the paper, holds it

up to a nearby lamp and spots some kind of writing on it,

"Paul's going to love this one...

right up his alley."

Pulling out a small plastic bag, he squeezes it open and places the

evidence into the bag,

"What did I say? Detectives mother-fucking detect!"

Chapter 15

Ellen's teeth chatter in response to a late March snowstorm that's socked-in the whole Tri-State area. She's just finished shoveling the last of her front steps as Sam the mailman comes a calling,

"Morning Ms. Carpenter."

Sam's wrapped from head-to-toe in a one-piece snowsuit that seems well suited for an Antarctic gale. All that's visible is a patch of dark brown cheeks and his infectiously warm smile,

"They've got you working on a day like this Sam?"

"You know me Ms. C...be it rain, snow nor dark of night."

Ellen smiles as Sam hands her the daily postal allotment, then with a motherly tone warns Sam,

"Be careful sweetie...not everyone is as diligent as I

am with their stairs and walkways."

"And a fine job it is my lady."

Sam then clicks his heels,

"Off to finish my appointed rounds."

She does a curtsy then in her best Scarlett O'Hara impersonation,

"Why, thank you sir" she waves her hand back

and forth like a fan. "I declare, I certainly do rely

on the courtesy of strangers."

Sam slaps his glove on his knee and lets out a belly laugh,

"You make a day of work totally bearable Ellen...

you really do."

She smiles,

"Off you go young man...we'll see you soon old

friend."

As he sets off to his appointed rounds she smiles and remembers

something about Tommy,

"Sam...that was Tommy's self-proclaimed nickname...

I haven't thought of that in years."

Ellen begins the ascent back to her warm abode, shuffles through her

morning delivery on the

way up the stairs and notices an official looking document amongst the
junk mail. She brings that letter

to the top of the pile...it's labeled,

OFFICIAL: STATE of NJ/ DEPT of FAMILY HEALTH

AND WELFARE.

Standing at her top step with some silly-letter shouldn't make her heart
race, but she knows this must

be the official-mandate Sophia was telling her about,

"C'mon silly...Sophia's right...it'll be good

for ya."

But the thought of having to relive the pain of losing Tommy...with some

probing doctor and a cast of strangers simply mortifies her. She enters the

front door, completes her disrobing then rips into the letter,

Dear Ellen Carpenter,

It's with the heaviest of hearts that we send our deepest

condolences for the loss of your child.

But, in accordance with Mandate #1232a, Section 4368

of the Health and Welfare in the Workplace Act, should

you chose to return to your current employment

position,

(3) Group Session are required. SEE BELOW for

MANDATED THERAPIST and commencement

date.

Session Date: 04/01 5:00 pm

Group Session Therapist: Dr. Jeffery Alton.

She takes a sip of her coffee,

"Oh, now that's rich...April Fool's Day."

She rubs her temples and stretches out the kinks built up from shoveling

for the last hour and a half,

"Who knows...maybe some shared grief will

be cathartic."

Ellen takes her mug and heads off to her bedroom to get the rest of her

day started.

Chapter 16

Sitting alone on the sofa in her den, Alexis turns the page of her mother's "Official Weinstein Photo Album". The photo album was sadly one of the few salvageable items from that horrible crime scene Alexis had once-called a childhood home.

A photo of her parents gazing at their two-month old bundle of joy at first makes her smile...but the sadness of her new orphanage becomes overwhelming,

"Mommy...Daddy...what am I going to do

without you?

Alexis rubs her temples vigorously, attempting to calm herself as a facial-tic contorts her jawline,

"Relax and breathe Alexis."

She takes her own advice, takes a few deep breathes then reopens the photo album to her "High-School Years" section. She covers her eyes in shame upon viewing her "Prom Pictures",

"Breathtaking!"

That's Alexis' recollection of what her father had shouted, right before snapping the photo of her in that hideous tangerine-colored dress,

"Breathtaking...hmm?"

She laughs sarcastically,

"No, you weren't too biased were you Daddy?"

Glancing downward at the coffee table and seeing her own reflection, she

strokes her auburn hair while adjusting her size 16 jeans,

"Ordinary, yes. Average, C + and middle of the pack,

definitely...but breathtaking?"

Alexis tilts her head to the side,

"If only the rest of the world saw me through your

eyes Daddy."

Going through her mom's album has given Alexis something to hold

onto...something with a fond memory for a change. Not the stench of

three-day-old death...just a simple, friendly port in the storm and

somewhere to hang up insanity's hat, if just for a moment.

While turning to the album's next page, a loose picture slides out

of its place and into her lap.

"Alexis and Cousin Peter" is written on the back side.

The painful memory of being stood-up that evening brings-on another

facial tic,

"Mommy...why wouldn't you just have let me been

stood-up that night...just left well enough alone.

Why, oh why did you compound my misery by forcing

second-cousin Peter to take me to prom?"

After reapplying the dislodged picture, she notices a group-shot

photograph of her family all smiling together on that same prom night.

Bringing the album near to her chest, Alexis shuts her eyes tightly and

begins to cry.

"Enough of that crying shit" Alexis proclaims while

wiping the tears from her eyes.

She flips to the next page of the album, spots a faded black and white

photo of her father, as a child. Standing proudly next to her father in the

circa. 1940's picture is her fraternal grandparents,

"How did you do it Daddy?"

Alexis thinks back to all the stories her dad would tell of Nazi Germany

just before the war,

"All of that death and persecution...just for being a Jew."

Removing the photo from the album, she flips it over and sees,

Baby: Maxwell Weinstein//Parents: Ira and Gladys

Weinstein

Date: Oct. 1934

Reversing back to the image,

"I can't even imagine what you went through Daddy.

It's tough knowing that you're both gone."

She kisses the photo,

"But to see your own parents, when you were only five

or six, stripped naked at the Auschwitz gates."

Fondly eyeing the images of her grandparents,

"And to see them shot dead by those animals...

right in front of you as they dragged you away."

She begins to cry but then catches herself,

"You didn't have any power then Daddy...

but I do now. I will avenge what you couldn't."

Placing the photo atop of the Hebrew Bible that sits on her coffee table,

she raises them to her chest and recites,

"I remember all of what you taught me Daddy.

Revenge is mine sayeth the Lord. Deuteronomy 32:35

To me belongeth vengeance and recompence;

their foot shall slip in due time: for the day of their

calamity is at hand, and things that shall come upon

them make haste."

Chapter 17

Monday's madness at the District Attorney's office has a steady stream of activity past Sophia's desk. The comings and goings of a busy day has the better part of the morning already gone...Then came that package.

Sophia leafs through Scott's inbound deliveries, trying to weed through the junk mail when something takes her by surprise,

"Something addressed to me?"

Scanning the manila envelope, she notices the return postage has only the City and State listed,

"Hmmm...New Haven, Connecticut. Scott's

investment property is up in New Haven."

But, as loyal subordinate should, she sets the mystery package aside and finishes the chore of sorting the Big Guy's mail. Her anticipation comes to a boil by the fifth letter,

"Awe screw-it...I gotta know...

and only one way to find out."

Sophia takes the mystery package and opens the folder's prongs. She grabs her antique Tiffany & Co. letter opener then carefully finishes off the sealed portion. After sliding the letter opener back into the sheath,

she reaches in and pulls out the envelope's contents,

"My my....how interesting...a handwritten

letter."

Sophia grabs the reading glasses from her desk, slides them on and takes

notice the letter is written in a familiar pen to her eye,

My Dearest Sophia,

Normally, a simple salutation as this letter contains, would bring a

cheerful smile...but THIS letter is from Tommy...it simply floored her at

"My Dearest Sophia".

Scrambling to catch her composure, Sophia looks to the bottom of

the page. Tommy's familiar sign-off confirms her first impressions,

Always yours,

Tommy C.

She sits in wonderment,

"How...how..?"

Sophia ponders, trying to come to grip with Tommy's post-mortem parcel.

"You little scamp...you've been playing these tricks on me since I

first met you."

Sophia reads from the beginning,

My Dearest Sophia,

My dear my dear, it is all so clear,

I need your help, there's no need to fear.

For spring has near sprung and the Ides

 have just past,

My joyous news is impending and sister

it's coming fast!

With that being said...and for now only that

I am enlisting you Sophia...my dearest confidante.

It's my shell and pea game, from equinox to near

Solstice.

Two more clues will be coming...oh shit, I can't

think of anything that rhymes with solstice...Lol

Wait, I got it...you're the woman with the

most-est.

Love You Sophia!!!

Always yours,

Tommy C.

A mixed bag of emotion overwhelms Sophia's senses as she sits stunned,
"How did you send this to me Tommy? And two

more clues...what can that mean?"

After snapping out of her fog she declares,

"Ellen...I gotta call Ellen."

Sophia grabs the phone, dials Ellen's number and by the fifth ring, it feels

like an eternity. The voicemail picks up,

"This is Ellen Carpenter...leave a message...Beep."

"Ellen...its Sophia...please call me ASAP...something

crazy just happened...don't freak...

its good news...Love you."

Sophia hangs up the phone, takes a Manila envelope from her desk and

fans herself with it.

Chapter 18

Dr. Paul Carol is peering through his microscope when he first hears Derrick's robust voice reverberating from down the Crime-Lab hallway. He's just finishing up one of the investigatory projects upon today's busy docket and knows what's coming along with Derrick's booming voice, a big favor. The gang's laughter comes to a crescendo so Paul quickly taps in some final results on his computer.

Derrick's tall frame fills the doorway as Paul waves him over to his work area,

"Paul my man, how's tricks kid?"

Derrick quickly walks over and they share a brotherly hug. Derrick, who stands a good six inches taller than Paul, playfully rubs the top of his buddy's head. Paul returns the favor with a few well-placed jabs to Derrick's ribs,

"It's kicking Detective...how's your hairy

bean-bag hanging?"

Derrick laughs at Paul's quip but switches emotional gears,

"Paul...I need a big favor buddy."

"Don't sweat it D...I've already recreated the note

and was sending it to your Computer."

"What ya got for me Paulie?"

Dr. Paul finishes tapping in a few more entries on his computer,

"After running your evidence through the

spectrometer and using the re-creative program

that I've just finished for the Department...

got ya some interesting results. Just putting on the

finishing touches...we should have an answer in a

second."

Paul gestures for Derrick to dim the lights,

"Check out the overhead screen Derrick."

Derrick complies and seconds later, a blurry image appears on the

elevated screen,

"Once I pinpoint the correct wavelength, the

precipitate should just jump off the paper."

Paul reaches over and adjusts a nob on his apparatus. Derrick stares

keenly up at the large screen as the image, printed in a pen, slowly comes

into focus.

lippe-LeSe

Paul finishes his program's tweaking and shouts,

"Now that's what I'm talking about...

asked for and delivered! Don't know what

the hell it means...but there it is my brother."

Derrick jots a few tidbits into his notebook,

"That's fuckin' huge Paulie. Look...it's obviously

written in a woman's-hand and check-out the

large feminine loop to her L's". I think Sylvia

was trying to drop us a hint."

Paul studies Derrick's face...he's seen his old-friend's talents on display

before,

"Keep going with it Derrick...you're on a roll."

Derrick's eyes are ablaze with a contemplative-fire as he snaps his fingers,

"I've got it...she must have heard them talking

to each other before they killed her...then

scribbled down their names for me to find."

He smiles then high-fives Paul. Derrick pulls out his wallet, flips it open to

reveal the photos of Sylvia, Max Weinstein and Tommy,

"Here's Max and Sylvia right next to

Thomas Carpenter."

He points to Tommy's picture then flips to the next photo,

"And here's one of Sally Tithes."

Paul fraternally slaps Derrick on the arm,

      "Ever since we were kids Derrick...

      you've been a mixture of a crazed pit-bull

      with the compassion of Mother Theresa."

Derrick leans-in closer to Paul,

      "When I take a case Paulie...it becomes more

      than personal. I want to attack it as if they were...

      well, you bro. That twenty-four/seven day burn

      that won't stop eating at me...so they ARE my

      family and they WILL stay in my wallet until it's

      over. I've transferred twenty-two pictures over

      to my "Solved Album"...and I'll be damned if I

      fail here."

Paul looks at overhead screen,

      "Way to go Mrs. Weinstein."

Derrick looks at her photograph,

      "Damn straight Paulie...Sylvia's my girl."

Chapter 19

There's a lavender crocus outside Quincy White's apartment, nestled between two melting slush balls...leftovers from the other day's substantial snowfall. Quincy locks his front door, takes notice of the flower and bends down to inhale the first scent of spring,

"Spring has finally sprung!"

He adjusts his tie and straightens his Bank of America insignia pin,

"This is going to be a great day. The sun's

shining and I think I even hear a bird singing."

Arriving at his Altima he jumps into the driver's seat, looks into the rear view mirror and adjusts it to check himself out,

"What do you think Mr. Wonderful...

is this gonna be a great day or what?"

He reaches into his ashtray and pulls out a perfectly rolled marijuana joint,

"Ahhhhh, my sweet-smoking mama-jamma

for after work...doesn't get much better."

Quincy re-evaluates his look in the mirror and comes-up with a bright-idea. After opening the glove compartment, he pulls out a spray bottle of cologne and drops it onto the passenger seat,

"Maybe just a quick poke or two...

for my ride into work."

He slides the doobie between his lips, turns the ignition key and after sparking the joint, recklessly speeds his Altima out of the parking space...which is followed by the metal-twisting smash of his Nissan directly into a just-passing Police Patrol Car.

Moments later, the steady pounding of a policeman's black flashlight on his roof and vague gray shapes are the only thing Quincy can make-out...as he struggles to find his consciousness.

"UNLOCK THE DOOR OR WE'RE SMASHING IN

THEWINDOW IN ASSHOLE!" shouts an officer.

The sharp stinging in his left eye reorients Quincy to his surroundings. He rubs his temple and notices through his squinting that his right hand is doused with blood. A sight that finally brings him back to REALITY...

...the REALITY where you just T-boned a police cruiser.

...the REALITY where you're still harboring a

smoldering joint between your lips AND you're

carrying more than your fair share of outstanding

warrants.

...the REALITY where a second officer has just smashed

open your window, dragged your ass out of the car and

you're face-first down on the pavement.

Quincy, now lying handcuffed and in the back of an ambulance with a

police escort, looks up at his paramedic and softly mumbles,

"I thought this was really gonna be a great day."

The police officer laughs at the ironic statement as Quincy slips back out

of consciousness.

Chapter 20

Ellen sits upon her living room sofa staring at Tommy's letter. She re-reads the letter, then with frustration calls into her kitchen,

"I just don't get it Sophia...first of all, how did

Tommy actually get it mailed...and what could

he be trying to tell us?"

Sophia arrives with a cup of tea and sets it down on the coffee table,

"Here you go sweetie.

Sophia takes a seat on the other end of the sofa,

"I've been racking my brain about that."

Ellen slowly traces Tommy's written word with her finger,

"He still has the same handwriting as

when he was a little boy...see how his

print and incursive are written together...

that's an indicator of genius."

Ellen puts the letter down on the coffee table then runs her hands through her hair,

"From equinox until six weeks pre-solstice...

that's spring until almost summer...hmm."

"Okay...let's do the math...Tommy had to

have it setup before he came home from

college...mid-December before..."

Ellen catches Sophia off-guard as she claps her hands together,

"I've got it...he was going to surprise me.

Tommy knew how much I wanted him to

graduate this May. He must have worked it

out with his professors. Tommy wasn't

scheduled to graduate until the following

semester...and Yale's cap-and-gown ceremony

is set for May."

Sophia nods her head,

"Damn Ellen...maybe when you come back to

the office full-time, we'll put you to work with

the detectives."

Ellen waves-off Sophia's praise,

"I swear, I'm no super-sleuth...Just have been

dealing with Tommy's super-brain for so long ...

I know how he thinks."

"You're probably right honey...we'll just see if

we can put together the few pieces that we do

have to this puzzle. It sounds very plausible

though."

Ellen takes a sip of her tea,

"That's gotta be it."

A determined looks comes upon Ellen's face,

"But what I'd really like to do...

is to find those murders myself

and..."

Sophia interrupts,

"And do what honey? Take 'em out?"

Ellen instantly understands Sophia's objections,

"Ellen, I understand the temptation to

take things in your own hands."

She places her hand on Ellen's shoulder,

"You know better than most how it

works. Victims who get involved get

hurt."

Grabbing her younger counterpart on both shoulders, Sophia gently

spins Ellen so they face each other,

"You've also been working with Detective

Hayes...he's the best in the business."

Ellen smiles then nods in agreement,

"I know...I just get so frustrated with

doing nothing to help."

Sophia lightly grasps Ellen by the chin and sympathetically nods,

"I know honey. But Scott told me that a

couple of the pieces to the puzzle have

finally fallen into place. These are some

terrible guys Derrick's dealing with."

Sophia picks up her tea, takes a sip and settles into the couch,

"Plus, we have the Big Guy taking point

on the logistics of the investigation."

Ellen's eyes tellingly sparkle upon hearing Scott's reference...and it

doesn't go unnoticed by an ever-mindful Sophia.

"You saw Scott sneaking a peek at you...

when you came into the office the other

day, didn't ya?"

Ellen coyly grins,

"C'mon now Sophia...I've been a paralegal there for years and he's never even taken notice of me before."

Sophia scoffs,

"Yeah right...hidden glances are Scott Phillip's specialty...if I could only get the two of you kids together."

Ellen sweetly stops her oration,

"Sophia, it's been so long since I had any stirrings like. I don't think that I could ever restart that flame. And now that Tommy's gone..."

Sophia again grasps Ellen's hand,

"That's exactly my point sweetie. I could only imagine the torture of losing your baby. But what did Tommy always say to you... about once he left for college?"

Ellen begrudgingly replies,

"That's when I promised him that I'd get

back out there and meet someone special."

Sophia slaps her own knee,

"Exactly...Now I'm not looking for you two

kids to fall in love overnight...but do you find

Scott attractive?"

Ellen playfully scratches her chin,

"Hmmm...he's big, successful, pretty darn cute...

I would say a resounding yes."

"He's obviously attracted to you Ellen. I saw his

jaw hit the floor when he noticed you in that

black dress the other day."

Ellen waves her off,

"Cut it out silly. I did look pretty damn

terrific though."

"Just think about it honey...and promise to

just let the guys deal with the rough stuff...

okay?"

Sophia holds up Tommy's letter,

"We've got our own mystery to solve."

Chapter 21

The huge black rear-door of "Club Wave Street" opens violently, nearly knocking Luc Detaille' to the asphalt. He staggers backwards in avoidance and luckily is snared on the arm by the surprisingly nimble 300 lb. doorman,

"That was close little brother" bellows the behemoth.

Luc regains his composure, tucks in his dress shirt then slaps his friend on his arm,

"My man Big Tiny...you're always looking

out for me."

They enter the club's back hallway leading through into the kitchen area and the slamming of the giant metal door startles Luc. Big Tiny grabs his buddy tightly on both shoulders and with genuine concern asks,

"What's up with you Luc? I've never seen

you so damn jumpy."

Big Tiny thinks for a second, then roars,

"Okay...whose ass am I squashing?"

"Just a few things off kilter Tiny, no worries...

You've seen brother Philippe tonight?"

Big Tiny shakes his head yes,

"He came in about an hour ago...

still in the back-lounge, I think."

"Thanks Tiny for the info...stay cool."

Luc turns then makes his way into the club.

Seated at a dimly lit table near the rear of the club's lounge is Philippe, seemingly unfazed by the hundreds of partygoers. Luc notices Philippe as he attempts to weave through the crowd,

"Philippe...Philippe!"

His barking falls on deaf ear as he walks straight into a lovely mocha skinned girl in a shimmering dress. He accidentally knocks her martini glass to the ground,

"I am so sorry" fumbles a nervous Luc.

He seizes the moment to take advantage of the situation and slides closely to her ear,

"How bout we grab a back table...I'll have

the bartender rustle up a bottle of the

bubbly my love?"

Shaking her head no, Luc then gulps, feeling a large hand grab his shoulder. He is quickly spun around and standing in front of Luc is a large man in a tailored suit. They meet eye-to-navel and Luc stammers,

"Sir...please, I had absolutely no

intentions..."

The well-dressed monster reaches around Luc and hands a new martini

glass to his sweetheart. He nods his head to her, grabs Luc by each

shoulder blade and lifts the dangling Haitian up to his face. Luc hangs like

a rag doll as the giant stares directly into his eyes. Luckily, his saving grace

arrives as the diminutive girl says,

"It was an accident Bernard...he just

asked if he could replace my drink."

The large fellow glances at his girl, then back to Luc,

"No problem then my tiny friend."

Luc is placed carefully back to the ground,

"Hope I didn't scare you little man."

Luc doesn't look back at the couple as he hastily makes his way over to

Philippe, finally reaching the table,

"Did you see that Philippe?"

Luc slides into the booth,

"That man coulda killed me."

"We've got more important fish to

fry my brother."

He points towards the V.I.P. balcony,

> "Too many god-damned coincidences
>
> in one fucking day...that shit speaks
>
> volumes to this Port-Au-Prince child."

Philippe raises his pointer finger,

> "First...I've received info that the police
>
> have our dear friend Quincy's in custody...
>
> Cousin Renee says that Q-mon is looking
>
> to make a DEAL with the cops to save his
>
> own worthless ass."

Philippe pulls him near,

> "We're both aware of Quincy's big-fucking
>
> mouth and his tendency to crack under
>
> pressure."

Luc sits befuddled, not connecting his brother's dots,

> "Think Luc...what's the one poker chip Quincy
>
> could cash-in with the Police?"

Luc thinks for a moment,

> "The ice Philippe...that diamond ring in our
>
> freezer and our year-long stash of loot."

Philippe nods in agreement then holds up two fingers,

"And look up to eleven o'clock...see our

partner-in-crime LeSean, hanging with those

beautiful women on the balcony. He's

ordering bottles of Cristal like their going

outta style...and here I thought we were all

in the same poor-house until our haul made

it down to Philly for pawning."

Luc's now completely cued into the plot,

"So...what's our next step Philippe?"

Philippe taps his fingers on the table top,

"I need to think...got this terrible feeling

LeSean is gonna try and fuck us outta our

share of the money and screw Cousin Renee."

Philippe notices Luc's nervous fidgeting,

"Don't worry little brother...I'll get it ALL handled."

Chapter 22

On the way driving over to her first appointment with Dr. Alton, Alexis' navigational app on her phone informs her,

"Next turn in five-hundred feet...your final

destination will then be two-hundred feet

on your right"

Her radio-station then returns to play over the Ford Fusion's speakers,

"Well New Jersey...its 4:50 and you know

what that means..."

A loud steam whistle, signifying work's end, blears over the speakers,

"That means all of you need to...GET BACK TO

WORK! April Fool's you knuckleheads."

The navigation system reaffirms,

"You have reached your final destination."

Alexis pulls her Fusion into a spot in front of the large, but modest looking Dr. Alton's home/office. She turns the car off then settles back into her seat...unsure of her next move.

After deciding this whole "share your feelings and release the grief with Dr. Alton" is a horrible idea, she resets her navigation system for back home. Just then, a silver-haired nurse waving near the top of Dr.

Alton's front steps catches Alexis' eye. She slides the key out of the

ignition and opens the door,

"C'mon Alexis...nothing but healing

going on here" the older woman calls out.

Alexis is startled...how does this unrecognizable figure know her name?

The woman descends the steps and Alexis reflexively waves,

"Hello Alexis...I'm Mrs. Duval. Doctor Alton's

so pleased you could make it. Please follow

me dear so we can get things started."

A still startled Alexis stammers,

"Okay...sounds good."

She puts an arm around Alexis' shoulder,

"Now let's get the ball rolling young lady."

They quickly ascend the steps then enter the house.

Dr. Alton enters his Patient Waiting room, spots Mrs. Duvall

reviewing some paperwork with Alexis then walks over to the nurse's

station,

"Hello, I'm Dr. Jeffrey Alton."

He reaches and gently shakes Alexis' hand,

"And you must be Alexis...the pleasure's all

mine."

Mrs. Duvall calls over to a woman sitting in the waiting room reading a magazine,

"Ms. Carpenter."

Ellen removes her attention from the magazine and looks over at Mrs. Duvall,

"The doctor will see you now."

Mrs. Duvall turns and says to Jeffrey,

"Mrs. Foster will not be attending today's

session doctor...the flu's what she said."

Dr. Alton shrugs his shoulders,

"Never-no-mind...a group is from two to

two-hundred twenty-two. Mrs. Duvall,

will show you the ladies the way to the

Healing-Room...I'll be there in just a moment."

He nods accordingly then exits the office through the door leading to his residence.

Mrs. Duvall waves for them to follow,

"C'mon girls, I've already set-up everything

for your first session."

They follow her through the door and into the Healing-Room, where their

eyes are drawn to that special red couch. Mrs. Duvall has the cushions

pre-set just so...ten or so pillows laid out strategically to separate the two

ladies, into their own comfort-zone.

"Okay, let's make ourselves comfortable

and take a seat."

The girls make direct eye-contact for the first time. Ellen breaks the ice,

"Kinda feels like the first day of class...

not exactly sure of where to sit."

Alexis gestures that she'll grab the right side of the couch.

"Anything to drink girls?" asks Mrs. D.

They both decline as Dr. Alton enters the room and they take their

respective seats. Jeffrey settles into his plush leather chair, directly facing

the duo as Mrs. Duvall places a fresh can of Coke next to him,

"Ellen, Alexis...I realize you both work for

the State and that you're both required to

be here, as terms of your reapplication of

employment. With that being said, that's

definitely NOT what this is about...this is a

simple form of psychotherapy that is about

YOU. Our aims are modest...helping YOU cope

with the grief and mourning following the death

of your loved ones. It's not uncommon to feel

withdrawn from friends...to feel utterly hopeless

and helpless...and the ANGER that inevitably

follows."

Alexis and Ellen are engrossed as the Dr. continues,

"Some people laugh uncontrollably,

some can never seem to be able to shed a

tear...and some feel a self-loathing for not

actually being there to save that special

someone. You can expect a wide range of

emotions ladies...but rest assured in this,

I believe in my heart of hearts...if you share

that grief with someone of like experiences,

in a warm and inviting setting and circumstance,

you WILL receive the support that your Psyche

not only longs for, but must have in order to

survive. Then, and only then will you find a

semblance of resolution."

Dr. Alton pauses as the ladies squirm a bit in their seats, overwhelmed by his oration. Sensing their unease, he soothingly states,

"In a nutshell...you put in a penny of sharing

then you'll take out a pound of healing. Now

whether that turns out to be some emotional

closure...or just being able to handle a full day

of work without wanting to run and hide...

we WILL find a safety zone...together."

The ladies both smile warmly as Alexis shakes her head yes,

"I'm in Dr. Alton."

A moment later Ellen sincerely adds,

"Me too Doc...I'm all-in. Let's get started."

Jeffrey taps on his notebook with his pen and warmly smiles,

"Well then...let's get started indeed."

The ladies look at each other, then at Dr. Alton, unsure of how to begin.

He reassuringly states,

"I've always found that the best way to start...

is to actually start. So here goes...My story.

It's one that begins and ends with my own

personal unresolved guilt.

Guilt is a demanding and unforgiving mistress...

It's contemplative as "to be or not to be",

but real as a punch right in the kisser."

He takes a sip of his Coke as the atmosphere begins to ease,

"When I first came back home from college,

out on Long Island, I decided to take a year

or so break from school. You know,

to recharge my batteries. That's when my

life's course would be altered...forever.

I saw HER, from across the room...

it was like a vacuum sucked the breath right

outta my lungs. I had known Christine ever

since childhood...we used to spend every

summer together at the Union Elks Swim Club.

Our dads were both founding-member Elks,

and along with about three hundred other

families from the neighboring towns. We

would spend these idyllic summer days

playing and swimming where our biggest

concerns were getting sat down on "the bench"

for running,...or complaining that it sucked

being too-young and having to leave the pool

for "Adult Swims".

Dr. Alton pauses and takes another sip,

"Kind of like a dream when you stop and think

about it. Every year since I was six and Chrissy

was five, we'd fall head-over-heels into our

Memorial through Labor Day Love. I swear,

some of the sweetest and purest emotions

ever shared by two young, star-crossed lovers.

Because as summer's do, they'd come to a

bittersweet end, then back to our respective

towns and lives. We shared shattered hearts

every Labor Day."

Sitting on the edge of her seat, Ellen urges him to continue,

"Okay, then what happened?"

Dr. Alton notices that Alexis is a bit less engaged than Ellen, so he directs

his attention to her,

"When I first had gone away to college,

I stopped coming back home for the

summers and Chrissy and I lost touch
but then that all changed as there she was…
at this little dive-bar called "Apples".
All five foot ten of her, with that jet black
hair and that crooked Italian nose standing
across the room…it was like a damn tsunami
hit me. And for the love of God, just like in
the movies, she slowly turned and saw me.
Everything and everyone else seemed to go
into slow motion. It was just us two in the
whole universe. Everything froze in place as
she walked over to me, and without a word,
we began to kiss."

Alexis sighs as Dr. Alton continues,

"I think it was five or six hours before we let
the rest of the world back in. We walked
everywhere around Kenilworth that night
and wound up back at her parent's house.
Since she was driven to the bar that night
by a friend and now already home, we

agreed to meet back up the next day

finally get to realize all of those plans

we had made."

Mrs. Duvall enters the room and drops off two glasses of water for the

girls. They both take a big swig as Dr. Alton continues,

"The next day came with so many

wonderful expectations. After working

my part-time job at this liquor store,

which coincidentally was in the same

strip mall as her father's bakery, Chrissy

picked me up in her Trans-Am. When I

tell you it was the most magical night of

my life, I'm understating it ten-thousand fold.

Down Kawameeh Park that night, in her

Trans-Am, wrapped in each other's arms

and making love for the first time together...

after waiting all that time for each other.

I remember looking up at the stars and

promising her that I'd grab everyone out

of the sky for her."

His face contorts with emotion,

"But then it happened…after dropping me off, saying hello to my dad and meeting my dog Tippy, Chrissy asked me for the fastest way to get home from my house. Without a thought, I sent her up a street that had a dangerous intersection….just because she was in a hurry to get home. She knew that her Mom would be worried…obviously pre-cellphone days,

He takes a deep breath,

"Later that same evening, on the way home from grabbing some beer, I saw this horrific looking accident at that corner. I remember saying to my friend Kathy, "I sure hope it's nobody we know." At work the next day is when I got the news, a bakery store patron came into my liquor store and asked if I knew Christine and told me what had happened."

The girls both gasp,

"After a mad dash to the hospital, I saw

Christine's mangled body lying motionless

on the bed. Tubes and monitors were

everywhere...but just when I thought my

heart couldn't sink any deeper, her mother

started to scream at me. I had told Christine's

sister what had happened the previous night,

and how guilty I felt for having told Chrissy the

easiest to get home. There I was, served-up

for her mother on a platter...the sacrificial

lamb."

Dr. Alton winces in remembrance of the pain,

"Get out of this room you murderer" she yelled.

"That drunken kid would have never slammed

into Christine if you didn't send my baby to

her death...you fucking murderer!"

Dr. Alton takes a breather from his purging as the ladies regroup

their emotions,

"That's my unresolved guilt ladies...and a

day doesn't go by that I don't feel the sting.

The rational side of me knows that I didn't

kill Chrissy...or our shared dreams. But

watching her mother sit in her Cadillac,

for the next two years at that very same

dangerous intersection and cry her eyes out.

I watched her father age twenty years in the

two weeks between the accident and her

burial. But it is also why I got into this

profession in the first place...lessening my

horrific pain through group sharing.

The gravity of Dr. Alton's words hits Ellen like a freight train and she

begins to sob,

"I did it! I sent my baby to his death

Dr. Alton!"

Alexis, overwhelmed by Ellen's outpouring, reaches over the pillows and

pulls Ellen closer. She cries out in pain as Alexis slides closer and gently

strokes Ellen's hair,

"I knew I shouldn't let him go out that night.

Who needs another pair of those god-damned

pink slippers anyway?

Why Dr. Alton...why did I send my

baby to his death?"

He pauses in thought for a moment,

> "That's what we're here for Ellen...to figure out
>
> why we hold onto self-deprecating guilt.
>
> Why we hold ourselves responsible for
>
> something that we really had no control
>
> over to begin with...Life's fickle fate."

Smiling at Alexis for her thoughtful compassion, Ellen grabs a tissue and wipes her tears away,

> "I'm so sorry Alexis...I've been hear
>
> babbling away and haven't given you
>
> any time to talk about you."

Alexis smiles back,

> "Never fret my dear new friend. The time
>
> for me to reveal my secrets will come,
>
> I'm just so glad I could be here for you."

Dr. Alton pauses from his note taking of their ongoing session, raises his head and notices the 5:51 on the wall clock from across the room. In his best Humphrey Bogart impersonation,

> "Looks like this is the beginning of a

beautiful friendship."

Ellen leans across the couch and touches Alexis' hand as Dr. Alton
continues,

"Fabulous...simply fabulous...in a mere

fifty-five minutes we've kicked open the

door. We're on our way to clearing the

threshold to some seriously shared

understanding."

He flips a few papers of their file then locates the appropriate
page,

"Regretfully ladies...the session's hour

is up. Are you both on for next week...

same time?"

They stand, hug then without hesitation state in unison,

"Definitely."

Chapter 23

While waiting at a red light in his Mercedes, Detective Hayes senses someone's eyes fixated upon him. He turns his head to the left, sees his own reflection in an Audi R8's passenger window and instinctively flashes his award-winning smile. The sports car's window rolls down...the raven haired beauty that's driving puckers her lips and blows Derrick a playful kiss. He grins and scratches his chin just as the light turns green...in an instant, her Audi speeds away.

"Computer...Please pull-up the

Sophia Miller audio-mail."

The Computer responds in a feminine voice,

"Certainly Detective Hayes."

A moment later, Sophia's voice is heard,

"Hi Derrick...this is no April Fool's joke...

the big Guy requests your handsomeness

in-person at the Mark Twain Diner.

his inference was very good news.

Some big-break in your case. Nine

o'clockish, okay darlin'."

The audio ends and Derrick slaps his hand on the steering wheel,

"That's what I'm talking about.

Computer please pull up Ms. Tamara

Fox's information."

The Computer interrupts,

"I've already taken the liberty of sending

Ms. Fox your customary bouquet of apology

flowers along with an explanatory note. I've

also rescheduled the rest of your evenings

activities...please take note that I'll have

your bath drawn at 7:15..anything else

Derrick?"

"That'll be all Computer."

Derrick steps on the accelerator and jets home to his Hoboken

brownstone. Gripping the soft-leathered steering wheel, he remembers

exactly what's afforded him all these luxuries,

"Thank you Grammy Wagner...

Computer, send Dr. Paul a note that

we gotta take the trip over to Short

Hills this weekend to visit Grammy.

"Done Sir...her favorite flower,

carnations sent as well?"

Derrick gently taps the dashboard,

"Great idea Computer...definitely

those green carnations she loves.

And some fresh Bing-cherries as well"

Remembering back to his childhood, Derrick smiles thinking of the first

time Paul and he met Grandma Wagner. Raising her own three grandkids after her daughter's death was tough enough...but add Derrick and Paul to the mix and it was always an uphill climb every month. That was until that fantastic day when Grammy's lawyer informed her that she came into a boatload of money from a distant relative. And true to her form, Grammy spread the wealth amongst her juxtaposed clan.

"Anything else Sir?"

"That's all Computer...thanks."

Shifting into overdrive, Derrick readies for the night's enticing events.

Chapter 24

Sophia blows the steam from the top of her tea cup, takes a sip

then nestles into Ellen's sofa. Calling into the kitchen for Ellen,

"So that girl Alexis was really

nice, huh?"

Ellen, carrying her own tea cup, responds as she enters the living room,

"Nice is not even close...you'd love her

Sophia, she's one of us. Geez, I've only

known her for an hour and change...

fast falling friends I guess. I haven't

opened up like that in forever."

Ellen sits then stirs her tea,

"Now tell me about what's going on at

work...something about Tommy's case?"

"Nothing much to tell yet...just know that

Scott has an important meeting with Derrick

tonight. The Big Guy's been very coy...even

with me. He was in teleconference all day

with the NYPD Commissioner about a

certain prisoner. Other than that, I'm in

the dark."

Sophia reaches out, picks up a chocolate chip cookie and takes a nibble,

"Enough of all that...tell me what went on

during your session. I believe that I see

a glimmer of hope in your eyes."

"You know what...I do feel better. When

Alexis and I first met at the doctor's office,

it was really awkward. Neither one of us

knew what to say...or how to act...but

then this beautiful soul, Dr. Jeffrey Alton,

reassured us both that there was no pressure

to say anything we weren't totally

comfortable with. "

Ellen breaks off a small piece of Sophia's cookie, then noshes it,

"Still, we couldn't seem to get started.

Then, Dr. Alton shared with us his heart

wrenching story of a lost-love from his past.

He wanted to show us that through sharing

his pain and guilt, we'd be more likely to

reveal our own...and sister was he right.

I cried like a baby Sophia."

She wells up with tears as Sophia strokes Ellen's arm,

"All of these terrible nightmares I've been

having...and all of the self-loathing Sophia.

How can I ever forgive myself?"

Ellen begins slipping-away into her familiar trance, but catches herself just

in time,

"No...not this time. I'm getting a handle on

this...and that's that."

Ellen sits-up tall in her seat,

"Doctor Alton said we should confront our

emotional-escapism head-on."

They walk into the kitchen together and head towards the kitchen table,

"That's dynamite, seems like you're taking

to counseling like a duck to water."

"Definitely...just a bumpy road ahead."

After guiding another wedge of cheesecake onto her own plate Sophia

asks,

"Another slice?"

Standing next to her refrigerator Ellen answers,

"One and done for me, thanks."

With both hands, Ellen strokes her midriff and in a bad Southern accent,

"Watching my girlish figure don't ya-know."

Ellen grasps her waist and shakes her hips back and forth. Sophia laughs then points to the bottle of liquor on the counter,

"How about another smidgen of Amaretto

on the rocks?"

Ellen snaps her fingers,

"Coming right up."

She grabs a few ice cubes, scampers over to the table then adds them to their glasses,

"Step one, complete...step two..."

Ellen snatches the Amaretto from the countertop,

"...is on its way."

She spins the large cap off then fills each glass three-quarters of the way. Sophia takes a healthy sip of the chilled Amaretto,

"So, about this Alexis...what's her story?"

Ellen places the bottle on the table and takes a seat,

"She seems to be such a sad soul. I felt so bad,

between Dr. Alton opening us up...and all of

my blubbering, she really didn't get time to

say much in session. We did sit in the waiting

room and talk for about a half hour afterwards.

I know she lost both her parents over the holidays.

They were her only family and sadly, I pretty

much think the only friends she had in the world."

Ellen takes a serious swig of her drink,

"She's a bookkeeper for the Rahway State

Prisons and if I'm right, very religious.

I think if I help her out of her funk then maybe,

just maybe, I'll drag myself along for the journey."

Sophia raises her glass and toasts,

"Here's to the Journey."

After clinking their glasses together,

"Sophia, you're staying over tonight, right?

Sophia is wonderfully surprised...it's the first time since Tommy's death

that Ellen's asked her to stay overnight.

"Of course I will honey...I'd love to stay. A good movie

and some popcorn sounds great."

Chapter 25

Echoes of a driving rain upon the Prison's metal roof reverberate throughout the cellblock's dank corridors. Being the oldest penitentiary in New York's penal system leaves this Prison susceptible to the harsh chill of a spring sleet-storm. The torrent's rhythmic beating has had a calming effect upon the Inmates, as nary a soul stirs in the after-midnight hours. That is all except for Frankie Botelli, who's scanning the cellblock's long corridor...its game time.

Frankie confidently strides his pencil-thin, 5'3" frame through Renee Batiste's cellblock door...a place few men dare to tread.

"Hi Renee" Frankie stammers.

"I got that information...just like you asked."

Renee Batiste is not a man to be taken lightly. The darkness of his skin only partially hides the grotesque scars traversing down each cheek of his gnarled face...a face weathered by the last twelve years in prison and staring-down two life-sentences for murder. His hulking presence and seriousness of gaze would send most men quickly afoot. In his deep rasping voice, Renee beckons,

"What you got for me Frankie?"

"It's all good Renee...I did just like you asked.

Renee nods in understanding.

"It went down just like you said Renee.

That Quincy guy was crying like a bitch...

calling out for his fucking mommy when

they first tossed his dumb ass into the hole."

Renee takes mental notes as his jailhouse-rat continues,

"About an hour later, they put him into the

Interview Room with his Lawyer...musta told

SOME story to that mouthpiece...cause an

hour later, I saw them walking out together,

arm in arm and all smiles."

Renee grimaces as Frankie continues,

"C.O. Carolan said that bitch is in Solitary...

until he meets with some Detective from

Jersey."

Frankie stares at a footlocker on the opposite side of Renee's cell, waiting

for a response,

"That's all I got for ya Renee."

Renee's mind is ablaze as he calculates his options. A distressed Frankie

gulps,

"Renee...do ya think..."

Frankie gestures with his eyes towards the footlocker,

"...we could finish?"

Renee nods his head then Frankie darts towards his booty,

"There's a bonus in there for ya Frankie.

Job well done."

Frankie grabs two small zip-lock bags from the footlocker and he spies

their white powdery contents,

"You are truly a gentleman Renee...

anything you need boss...anything."

Renee gestures for Frankie to depart then begins to dissect the valuable

new data.

"What to do...and who to use?" Renee

Contemplates.

Being a "lifer" leaves someone with endless time for calculating. It also

shrinks the pool of who you can really trust. He's narrowed his inner circle

to two trains of thought.

First and foremost is his family. The devotion and protectiveness

he lauds upon Luc, Philippe and Grannie...for someone with his past indifference to human life, is remarkable to say the least. He would do anything in his power to safeguard the little family that he has left.

But secondly, and nearly as important, is the iron-fisted protection of the illicit empire he's built from scratch while in the joint. His far reaching influence, both in and outside of the prison walls, has afforded him a very comfortable lifestyle. Snapping his fingers,

"Menoni...got that junkie already

over a barrel. Piece of cake."

Chapter 26

A bit earlier that same April 1st day, a young man speeds along on his motorized scooter. He darts through the bustling London, England traffic then turns onto William IV Street. Moments later, he guides his transport to a rest right in front of the Trafalgar Square Post Office. Retrieving two envelopes from a pocket inside of his windbreaker,

"Tommy...I miss you brother."

Scanning the first envelope, he sees his name written on the front..."Xavier". He opens the seal and begins to read,

X-man...I hope this letter finds

you well. I know your studies

abroad at Oxford haven't allowed

you much time for correspondence

since you left the States. Thanks again

for forwarding the letter over to my

mom. See you when you get back

next Christmas buddy!

---Tommy C

Xavier refolds his friend's correspondence then returns it to his windbreaker.

"Can't wait to see you too old chum"

Xavier says as he drops the second

envelope into a mail receptacle.

"Like you said...if I haven't heard from

you go forward with your plan as

scheduled."

He grabs hold of the scooter's handlebars, pushes the automatic starter then nimbly continues his way down the busy thoroughfare. Xavier's unaware of his friend's Christmas Eve fate...they had set-up this piece of Tommy's puzzle before last winter's break when Xavier was still in the U.S.

Tommy Carpenter strikes again!

Chapter 27

Scott raises his eyes from his smartphone after hearing Sharon the waitress call out,

"You need a topper on your java

Mr. District Attorney?"

Waving his hand over his coffee cup,

"No thanks...but do a favor for

me doll, would you? When you

see a tall, dark guy in an expensive

uit come in, send him my way."

She flashes an okay sign and jets back to the main section of the Diner. Scott's booth is located in a quiet, rear section of the Mark Twain Diner...usually reserved for larger parties. He scans his phone, notices the 8:47 on its face and taps the Recorder App on the phone's screen,

"Note to self...take Sophia's advice

and call Ellen Carpenter this weekend.

Take a shot and don't be a chicken-shit."

He laughs for feeling like a fifteen year old with a major case of infatuation,

"Here I am, deciding life and death

issues, and the first thing I think of is

"Wow", I finally found an icebreaker

with Ellen."

Scott refocuses and spots Derrick and Sharon,

"Delivered as ordered Sir..." she boasts,

"...and your hot chocolate will be here

in a jiffy Detective."

Sharon departs as Derrick takes his seat.

"Hot chocolate...wouldn't have pictured

that one Derrick."

Derrick adjusts his tie,

"Never could acquire the taste for coffee.

So boss, what's up?"

"That hunch you've been working on...

think we've finally found some of those

missing pieces you've been looking for."

Derrick's excitement causes him to nearly jump out of the booth's seat,

"Talk to me Big Guy?"

"I've been working with the New York

Department of Corrections all day.

What started out as some low-level

pot bust has yielded some very

interesting revelations about your

murders here in Jersey over Christmas."

Scott slides the next page of his digital notes and shows Derrick a photo of

Quincy,

"Quincy White...a two-time offender is

looking at strike three for his latest

fuck-up. I just wished his Public Defender

hadn't shown up so soon...he was set to

sing like a canary."

"Hold on a second, I want to take some notes."

Scott waves his hand for Derrick not to worry,

"I'm sending all of my notes to your computer.

In between Quincy's sobbing and ranting,

he blurted out about these liquor store

robberies and that some lady from Jersey

had her missing ring-finger in a freezer...

and he knew exactly where to find it.

About two hours later, his lawyer requests

a formal sit-down for this Sunday

afternoon...to discuss some kind of relocation

deal in exchange for his information."

Derrick scratches his chin,

"Excellent."

Sharon delivers the cocoa and drops off a menu as they dive head-first

into the next phase of the case.

"So, what's our next move Mr. D.A?"

"I've got it all worked out...there's a bigger ball of wax here than we originally thought. I've been coordinating with all of the Police Chief's across the state and that same scenario...a home invasion followed with a liquor store robbery, kept popping-up in my conversations."

Scott takes a sip of his now cooled-coffee, then continues,

"I think this Quincy guy may be the lynchpin to all of these unsolved cases. I'm sending you in there to meet up with him and do that voodoo that you do-do so well with interrogations.

Derrick points at Scott, and the boys take their cue

"Done."

Sharon comes back over to the table and the guys take their cue. They both order a big meal, knowing they have a full night of planning for Sunday's showdown.

Chapter 28

A loud rapping at the garden apartment door stirs Luc from his slumber. He stumbles off his futon, makes his way to the door and the Saturday morning sunshine nearly blisters his eyes. The incessant pounding sounds like the door is coming off the hinges,

"Luc, I know you're in there...

open the fucking door!"

"I'm coming...hold your god-

Damned horses!"

Luc walks over and just as he turns the lock, the door flies open and crashes him square in the chest. LeSean pushes his way past Luc and enters the basement apartment,

"Lil' man Luc...where's Philippe?

We need to talk...like now."

"LeSean, relax me bro...Philippe's

got it all covered. Come, sit and let's

smoke this lovely blunt I have for ya."

Luc picks up a pre-rolled joint and hands it as an olive branch to LeSean,

"Okay lil' man, I'll listen...better

be fuckin' good." barks LeSean as

he takes a seat on the couch.

Luc strikes a match then holds it up to ignite his peace offering,

"Philippe assured me Cousin Renee

has a plan to permanently silence

Quincy...already in motion as a

matter of fact. So please LeSean...

chill out brother."

A fuming mad LeSean slaps Luc's cheek,

"I'll be the mother fuckin' judge

of when to chill the fuck-out

little man."

Hearing the ruckus downstairs, Grannie's voice calls down to the

basement,

"What's going on down there?"

LeSean's eyes lock onto Luc's as he raises his finger to his mouth,

"Shhhh...just be cool little man."

Luc wipes a spot of blood from the corner of his mouth,

"No worries Dearie...just some horseplay."

"Good choice Luc...very good choice."

LeSean walks over to the freezer, swings open its door and searches for

the frozen finger,

>"Philippe's on top of his game LeSean.
>
>Cousin Renee had us move the loot
>
>when he heard of Quincy's stupidity.
>
>It's at the drop house."

LeSean calms down, knowing that Renee has everything handled.

>"That's right LeSean...like I said,
>
>it's all covered. Renee's got some
>
>dumb-ass in the joint to do our dirty
>
>work. Philippe's out scouting that guy's
>
>wife and kid as we speak. Jjust in case
>
>the asshole doesn't feel like cooperating."

LeSean lights the blunt, takes a deep drag then releases a massive cloud

of smoke,

>"That's good to hear."

LeSean stands, puts out the blunt then slides it behind his ear,

>"Just remember to tell Philippe.
>
>He and me need a sit down...
>
>got it?"

"You got it LeSean, as soon as

I hear from him."

Without another word, LeSean bolts out of the apartment as Luc finally

can exhale a sigh of relief. He grabs a towel and dabs his mouth again for

blood,

"I gonna kill that bitch if he ever

touches me again...like I'm some

fuckin' red-headed stepchild."

Chapter 29

The inviting sounds of bacon crackling and the rich smell of coffee welcome's Sophia to her Saturday morning hangover,

"Ugh...where am I?"

After rubbing her eyes and yawning, she regains her bearings,

"Oh yeah...at Ellen's."

From the kitchen, wearing her favorite apron and in full cooking-breakfast-mode, Ellen merrily calls out,

"Do I hear Sleeping Beauty

stirring in there? Rise and

shine...coffee's on."

Sophia drags herself off the couch, folds the comforter they had shared for movie-night, then laughs when some popcorn and a Goober falls to the carpet. She bends over too quickly grabbing the snacks,

"Oh...my head...coffee please" cries

Sophia upon staggering into the

kitchen, with her hangover in-tow.

Looking bright as a newly minted penny, Ellen turns from the stove and places a plate of extra-crispy bacon on the kitchen table. She spots Sophia and mockingly sings,

"Isn't she lovely...isn't she

wonderful?"

Sophia raises her bloodshot eyes and notices that Ellen is glowing,

"Sweetie...you look radiant this

morning...what's gotten into you

young lady?"

Blushing while filling Sophia's glass with orange juice,

"Sophia...you're not going to believe it.

Scott Phillips called me this morning."

Sophia gingerly takes her seat and mumbles under her breath,

"Oh sweet Lord...he finally took the

plunge."

Ellen continues with her story as she also sits,

"First we were talking about Tommy's

case...which has, according to Scott,

taken a fantastic turn. But then,

we just started yapping and laughing...

about nothing...it was awesome."

Ellen nibbles on a piece of bacon,

"Not sure about going out on an

actual "date" Sophia. "

With genuine concern on her face,

> "What will people say? Dating so
>
> soon after Tommy's gone?"

"People...what people? I'm your

people honey. And this person says

that it's not only okay...but the two

of you couldn't be better matched

than if I drew it up on a drawing board."

Ellen smiles,

> "Well that's good then...cause I already
>
> said that I'd meet him for dinner tonight."

Sophia finishes her orange juice,

> "That's fantastic Ellen...you'll just have
>
> to try the stuffed veal Val-Dostano
>
> over at Mario's Tutu Benne.
>
> Just one bite and you'll be in heaven.

Ellen scrunches her pretty face,

> "Sophia dear...HOW did you know
>
> that Scott was asking me out to

dinner at Mario Tutu Benne's tonight?"

Sophia stumbles for a response,

"I...I don't know what to say...

damn, now that's a first for me.

Can I plead the fifth?"

Ellen waves her hand that all's fine,

"Don't worry sweetie...Scott

already told me that you had

mentioned for him to call me.

They share a laugh then Ellen remembers,

"Oh yeah, the Big Guy asked me to

have you call him at two o'clock today.

He needs help coordinating something.

I think it's Detective Hayes' Sunday

meeting at the Prison."

Sophia glances at the time on the stove,

"Thank you sweet Lord...it's only

ten thirty."

After finishing-off a slice of bacon, Sophia smiles,

"Well...your outfit for tonight's date is not

just going to pick itself out...

let's go make you look memorable!"

Sophia's outburst aggravates her gentle condition as she wobbles trying to

stand. Ellen steadies her tiny shoulders and softly whispers,

"Fair enough...but let's do it

sloooowly...okay?"

Arm in arm, they gingerly leave the kitchen and head towards Ellen's

bedroom.

Chapter 30

Seated in his silver Camry, Philippe attentively stares at a house situated a hundred feet or so ahead on his left. He rechecks the address on his cellphone,

"676 Thoreau Terrace...Union,

New Jersey."

Stalking is where Philippe is at his best...it's why Cousin Renee picked him exclusively for this job.

The determined patience to wait, for what may seem like forever...but then at the exact moment, pounce and go right for the jugular.

While sitting patiently in his car, Philippe fancies himself a black panther hiding in a tree, ready to leap down and attack at any moment.

His morning of waiting has finally come to an end as he spots the front door of 676 opening. A woman and young child emerge...the Prey is now in sight. Picking up his cellphone, he presses the DIAL button then places it next to his ear. A voice on the other side of the phone asks,

"Cousin Philippe...Are we on?"

Philippe exits the car then starts walking up the street towards the mother and child,

"Yeah Cousin, I'm walking their

way right now."

The other side of the phone now comes into focus...it is Cousin Renee on a smuggled cellphone from his prison cell. Renee is sitting on his cot next to Ronnie Menoni, a heavy set Italian convict who is seriously twitching. Sweat pours from Ronnie as he desperately fidgets about, wondering what's next. With cold-hearted frankness Renee states to a terrified Ronnie,

> "Listen Menoni...face it...you
>
> fucked up royally."

Renee slaps Ronnie across the mouth then grabs him tightly by the throat,

> "When you killed that family driving
>
> drunk that night...You fucked up.
>
> Getting' hooked on my dope and
>
> not paying me homage...
>
> now you really fucked up my friend.
>
> You fuckin' OWE me."

Philippe violently shuffles Ronnie's wife into the front seat of her SUV. He quickly jumps into the back seat then brandishes his large blade to corral the woman's full attention. Philippe points the knife directly at her baby, already secured in her child safety seat.

"Got them right here...just where

you wanted Renee."

Renee snarls as he informs Ronnie,

"I know you're gonna do what

I say Menoni...but just in case you

get cold-feet, I've added two extra

incentives for you to consider."

Renee turns the phone for Ronnie to view; the terrifying sight of a knife to

his daughter's throat has Ronnie's complete devotion. He begins to

blubber and pleads,

"Anything Renee...anything you

need...just please don't hurt them."

Renee forcefully punches him in the ribs,

"I'm a fair man Ronnie, just do as

I say and no harm will come...just

follow the plans to the letter."

Reeling from the physical assault, Ronnie gasps,

"You got it Renee...anything."

After struggling to sit up, Ronnie grabs Renee's arm and begs,

"May I ask my wife something?"

Renee nods his head then Ronnie speaks into the phone,

      "I'm so sorry Paula...You and

      Jasmine okay?"

Renee grabs the phone out of Ronnie's hand,

      "I told you no harm would come

      to your family...my man will explain

      it all to your bitch wife...they'll be

      fine if you follow my instructions...

      now get outta my sight you fuckin'

      junkie."

Ronnie slinks off Renee's cot then shuffles towards the cell door. Renee

gestures for Menoni to wait a second. Leaning over his cot, Renee then

grabs a baggie of smack and tosses it over to Ronnie,

      "Relax Menoni...we're even now.

      This one's on the house."

Ronnie snares the junk in maid-air then quickly hides it in his shoe.

      "I'll have Frankie stop by and give

      you all the particulars. Your shit is

      on the line here Menoni...DO NOT

      disappoint me."

"Okay Renee...whatever you say."

Ronnie departs as Renee grins,

"Just like clockwork."

Chapter 31

That same crystal clear Saturday-morning finds Alexis alone at her house. Yesterday's session with Dr. Alston was fantastic, but it has lit a foreboding-fire under her...she's got something sinister brewing. Shuffling through her Dad's effects in search of some vital paperwork,

"There they are." Alexis says

having located their Life-Insurance

Policies.

She places the policies, along with the deed to her parent's house and other assorted stocks and bonds, on her desk and crunches the figures on a calculator. After a few minutes of diligent calculations, she slams her fist upon the desk,

"That's why I love math...

it's an exact science."

Unlike Ellen's response to yesterday's group session, Alexis' escapism has followed a much darker path.

Yesterday's repressed anger and bitterness has been transformed into a laser-focused determination for retribution. She double-checks the math then logs her conclusions on a yellow legal pad,

$ 1,173,212 Total Assets =

The Max and Sylvia Foundation

for Redemption

Alexis taps the pencil to her chin as a demonic-grin appears...The dye has

been cast!

"Now all I have to do is bide my

time...wait til someone makes a

mistake...then the time will be mine."

Alexis swaps the yellow pad for a manila file labeled,

Dr. Sydney Kaufman---Oncology/

Alexis Lauren Weinstein

Alexis surveys her Patient-File then glances at a photo of her parents,

"Mommy and Daddy, please help

me find the patience and grant me

the time...to avenge you."

Pulling a small MRI-scan of her brain from the patient-file, she then

focuses on the sizeable-mass that's circled in RED. No matter how many

times she reviews the scan, the words "Inoperable" with and arrow

pointing to the tumor makes her cringe,

"Time really is ticking in my head

Mommy...just got to hope for the

opportunity to make my plan work...

around the short-time that I have

left above ground."

A resolute Alexis stands placing her fist on the desktop,

"Starting right now."

Chapter 32

"Quincy, would you please stop

being so difficult." asks Dan O'Shea,

Quincy White's frustrated Public-Defender.

Quincy sits calmly as the young, wet-behind-the-ears attorney paces the

floor of the prison's interrogation room. He places his manacled wrists

upon the metal table,

"Patience is a virtue Mr. O'Shea...

Not one name...NOTHING more

until we meet with the Reps from

Jersey."

Realizing that his best legal advice has fallen on deaf ears, the

exasperated counselor yields,

"Fair enough Quincy...what are

our plans?"

A self-assured Quincy then leans back in his chair,

"Here's how I see it Counselor...

I've given you just enough to peak

their interest. Dangle out there that

I've got some tasty tidbits about those

awfully bad men that they're

desperately looking for."

O'Shea taps the notes of their conversation onto his IPad as Quincy

continues,

"First, it's actually a year-long

string of break-ins...then we'll

sprinkle in a few of my friends

liquor store jobs and carjacks,

and oh baby...if my calculations

are right, it'll buy me a fresh start

somewhere in Bum-fuck Arizona."

Dan stops his typing,

"That's all well and good...but I do

need SOMETHING concrete to seal

the deal for tomorrow's meeting...

they're not just going to take the

word of some two-bit pothead."

"You make a fair point...Okay,

inform them about the four carat

diamond ring set in a perfect

platinum setting...and for

confirmation, tell 'em that the

missing finger had red nail polish

on it."

Dan grimaces as he completes his notes then waves at a mounted camera,

signifying the guards that he's ready to leave.

"That should do it Quincy...

we're set for tomorrow at noon."

Two prison guards enter to escort Quincy out of the interrogation room,

"Twelve o'clock sharp Danny boy...

Don't be late partner."

Chapter 33

Philippe descends the staircase from Grannie's into his darkened apartment, illuminated only by Luc watching some television. Philippe walks towards the kitchen,

"What's this I hear some problem

today? Grannie said it sounded like

a herd of buffalo down here."

Luc shrugs his shoulders as Philippe opens the fridge and grabs a can of Natural Ice,

"Not trying to keep anything from

me...are ya Luc?"

"It was just a misunderstanding

Philippe...LeSean just..."

An angered Philippe interrupts,

"LeSean...what did that mother-

fucker have to do with it?"

Philippe turns on the kitchen's overhead light, revealing a hand-sized bruise across Luc's face. A now enraged Philippe shouts,

"That Scumbag is DEAD!"

He pulls out a large knife,

"Come into my house and

rough-up my family. Scare my

Grannie half-to-death will ya?"

Philippe brings the shiny blade near to his face, staring at its gleaming

luster,

"Up close and personal...from ear

to ear...slowly, so you feel it dig

deep into your flesh LeSean."

Luc cautiously approaches Philippe,

"What's the plan now big bro?

Are we gonna be okay?"

Philippe's temper subsides and he puts his arm around Luc,

"Got it all covered man, Renee

has the Quincy thing all handled

and this other shit...it's just

hastened my original plans for

wasting LeSean."

Philippe chugs the contents of his beer,

"Let's go play some futbol Luc...

I'll take France and you can be

dear-Haiti this time...okay?"

"Sounds good Philippe...thanks

for taking care of everything."

Philippe grabs Luc playfully around the shoulders then drags him over to

the game console,

"Like Cousin Renee said Luc...

just like clockwork."

The brothers settle in for a mad-session of gaming as the minutes click

away towards midnight, bringing a close to Saturday's tumultuous events.

Chapter 34

The Sunday sun breaks on what feels like the first real day of

spring. Ron Menoni basks in the early morning's first sunlight that's

shining through the iron-barred windows. Folding laundry is Ronnie's A.M.

Detail today; but his mundane chore is the furthest thing from his mind.

Just as Ronnie feels like his nerves are about to fray, Frankie

Botelli slides out of the shadows and quickly approaches him. Frankie taps

him from behind and whispers,

"This is gonna be quick Ronnie.

Your laundry detail is done at eleven...

take your thirty minute shit-shower-

and-shave break and when you get

back to your cell, the rest of your day

will be waiting there for you. Renee's

got it all planned-out."

Ronnie looks around to see if anyone else is afoot,

"How will I know what to do?"

The indicator-buzzer from one of the dryers loudly activates, startling

Ronnie,

"Easy there Menoni...your instructions

and a very special present will be taped

to the bottom of your bunk."

Frankie surveys the laundry room...no one is around. He nimbly darts back

into the dimness but says before departing,

"Just follow the instructions man...

got it all covered, right down to

the minute."

Frankie slips away as Ronnie turns and tends to the freshly dried clothing

in the machine. His mind races at the thought of carrying out one of

Renee's twisted plans...but he knows the alternative to saying no.

"I just got to suck it up and take

one for my team. Oh, my God...

how did I get into this shithole?"

Ronnie quietly sobs as he continues with his daily chore.

Chapter 35

The softness of that old pink robe against her cheek embraces Ellen this Sunday morning. After waking from last night's whirlwind of a date with Scott, she snuggles into the delicate fabric,

"How did I get into bed...

and my robe?"

Stretching out the remaining bits of her slumber, Ellen recalls the fun of being out with him. She giggles, remembering one of his jokes from the restaurant,

"Oh my God...he's so funny."

Nestling back into her blanket's security, she drifts-off into a sweet memory from last night...

...The memory of when their first appetizer at Mario's, the Mozzarella En Carozza, was placed at the table and their hands touched reaching for it...I think he blushed,

"He's so sweet."

...The memory of how tiny her hand felt in his, while they slowly danced in the back room of the restaurant to a softly playing jazz composition. Spinning her to the tender music, he then dipped her gently. Ellen felt the strength in his arms as he raised her slowly close to him, just like she was light as a feather. Pulling her in closer, he inadvertently squeezed Ellen just a bit too tightly, but she was stirred by his brawny physique.

"He's so tall and muscular."

...The memory of Scott gallantly opening the car door for her on the ride home. Of how she, totally out of character, slid close to him and planted their first shared kiss upon his lips. Of how when she opened her eyes from that beautiful connection, a flash of heat lightning lit-up the nighttime sky,

"Now that's a man."

She rolls over and notices that placed upon the pillow next to her, is a note. After grasping the hand-written scribe, she props-up a few pillows and begins to read,

Ellen,

For a learned man of schooling,

whose livelihood springs from the

wielding of his tongue, you have

remarkably left me speechless.

Customary civilities call for a brief

waiting period, but I think

I'd bust if we didn't at least

talk on the phone tomorrow.

Scooping you up in my arms

last night just felt so right.

It jolted my lonely heart into

beating once again. You said that

we might be meant for each other.

Cause we never once turned the

radio on during the whole ride home...

just chatted like a couple of great friends.

As I gently lay you down and kiss you

goodnight...I couldn't agree with you more.

P.S. Sophia will have my Sunday scheduled...

I'm sure that our call will be arranged.

                    Scott

With the glee of a teenager eyeing her first love-letter, she re-reads

Scott's touching passage. Just then, something comes to mind,

        "Sophia...gotta let Sophia know

        what happened."

Ellen grabs the phone from her nightstand then texts,

"Sophia...what a great night

out with the Big Guy...

gotta talk...ASAP!!!"

She goes to set the phone down but it vibrates in her hand,

"Ellen...I heard! Super busy...

I'll call you at noon."

Ellen texts her back in response,

"Fantastic...can't wait!"

Setting the phone back on the nightstand, she lies back down under the

covers,

"Just like you said Dr. Alton...

set some ME time aside for

a change."

She stares adoringly at Scott's letter,

"Can this really be happening

to me?"

Rolling over and onto her stomach, she wrestles not only for a

comfortable position, but with the thought of actually being happy and

"maybe" falling for this guy.

"Just slow your roll Ellen my dear."

But just then, from the distance to her living-room, she hears her grandfather clock chiming out nine o'clock. The deep rhythmic tolling drifts her back to an earlier nine in the morning at her house; the day Tommy first left for Yale...

...Ellen runs frantically around her house as Tommy waits patiently for her near the front door. His bags are all packed and he's ready for his ride up to Connecticut. The grandfather clock rings nine just as a car horn beeps from outside the house,

"C'mon mom...Xavier's already here."

She runs over to him, kisses him upon the cheek and leaves a lipstick mark,

"I'm sorry honey" Ellen says as

she wets her thumb then wipes

her kiss from his cheek.

"No worries mom...but it is time."

Ellen steps back and gazes at her master creation,

"Are you sure you won't let me

take you up to school? I really..."

He steps in close and hugs her,

"Ma, c'mon...just like we discussed...

even change for the better is still

unsettling. This is the first day of

my new chapter…like we agreed;

you can come up to school

ANYTIME you want after today.

But only if YOU do what you

promised…okay?"

Releasing their embrace Tommy holds onto each of her hands,

"I'll try sweetie…just not

sure if I can."

"Me neither mom…it's all

new for me to."

He smiles at her,

"And all kidding aside…not

to be weird mom, but if you

asked any of my buddies…

you're the hottest thing

since sliced white bread.

I won't even tell ya what

your "Crack on your buddy's

Mom" name is."

"Please Tommy...I'm so sad...

I could really use a boost

right now."

He laughingly shakes his head,

"Well...every mom's got one...

at least if you have a son you do.

There's my buddy Tim's mom...

Judy Judy, with the thirty-two

flavored booty. Then Frank's mom

is Marge Marge, her ass is as big as

a barge."

Ellen giggles and asks,

"What's mine, what's mine?"

Tommy can't believe he's telling his mom,

"You're Ellen Ellen, the watermelon...

just once slice will kill a felon."

While laughing, she jumps in and hugs him tightly,

"Thanks baby...I needed that."

Xavier's car horn blares out again,

"Gotta go mom. Remember…

a promise is a promise.

Nothing in the world would

make me happier than the

thought of you finding someone.

Maybe one of those lawyers

at your job?"

The car horn beeps again as Tommy's eyebrows rise,

"Promise?"

He grabs his bag and kisses her one last time…

…Ellen fades back to reality and while hugging Scott's note

whispers,

"I will Tommy…

A promise is a promise."

Chapter 36

-----The clank of Derrick's revolver against the side of the prison lockdown gun-case leaves him with an unsettled feeling. He laments that sentiment to Scott over the barely noticeable Bluetooth in his ear,

"Hate not having my piece Scott...

it blows being around all these

assholes without it."

Derrick shows his credentials to the attending Corrections Officer, grabs his briefcase and passes through the last in a series of gated checkpoints. From his home-office, Scott informs Derrick of the remaining information,

"This Quincy character has been

pushing his public defender around

a bit...trying to dribble us information

and make a deal. So I need you to

take quick control of the meeting

and put this asshole in his place."

Derrick continues making mental notes for his upcoming encounter,

"Got it bossman...

Bring down the fuckin' hammer."

"I'm going to let you work your

interrogation magic Derrick...

I'll be in your ear the whole way

and when the time's right,

we'll slam that door shut."

Derrick, accompanied by a Corrections Officer, reach their destination as

the C.O. grabs a large key from his pocket, unlocks Room #2's door then

they enter. With confidence, Derrick walks over to the table in the middle

of the room, places his briefcase upon the table top and readies for

Quincy's arrival.

"I'm all set Scott."

"Great...no pressure,

but it's all hinging on this."

Derrick leans back into his chair,

"Just bring the lamb to my

slaughter...this lion will take

care of the rest."

-----Renee Batiste is reclined upon the bunk in his cell, idly reading a copy

of Dostoyevsky's "Crime and Punishment" and seemingly without a care in

the world. While adjusting his reading glasses, Renee catches sight of

Frankie outside his cell's door. Frankie leisurely walks on by, touches his nose twice and nods in Renee's direction...everything's been readied in Ronnie's cell.

Renee refocuses on his book then sinisterly chortles with the knowledge that his well-constructed plan will soon be bearing fruit.

-----A now cleanly shaven Ron Menoni cautiously enters his cell, scans the room, then again the cellblock to make sure that he's all alone. He walks over then lifts the thin mattress, discovering the items Frankie had taped to the bottom of his cot. Pulling off the taped note, he unfurls it and begins to read,

Follow this plan Menoni to the letter

and your whole family will be fine.

Take the small metal flask that's

taped here and follow the

instructions below. I don't care

if you have to shove them up

your ass to hide them...DO NOT

fuck this up Ronnie...your daughter's

life hanging in the balance.

Memorize this all quickly then

eat this note or I swear I'll have

your wife's teeth strung on a

chain around my neck.

Ronnie shuts his eyes and cringes at the thought of his family's

torture...he can read no more. It sickens him to think of the road he's

traveled to reach this point, so he runs to his toilet and vomits. Sitting

upon the cold cell's floor, he wonders if he actually has the nerve to go

through with Renee's plan. As he wipes the spew from his mouth,

Ronnie's stark reality comes into focus...he's about to kill someone to save

his family.

He reaches over, grabs Renee's instructions from the floor and

begins to commit them to memory.

-----A supremely confident Quincy struts around his cell. He finishes

making his bunk with the self-assurance that this will most likely be his

last day here.

"Just fold their feet to the fire

Q my boy...they'll be eating outta

your mother fuckin' hands before

ya know it."

A large C.O. approaches his cell's door,

"Time to go you piece of shit."

Quincy sharply quips back,

>"Oh yes...a piece of shit now...
>
>but in a mere few hours my
>
>good man, I'll be whistling Dixie
>
>somewhere out west...while you,
>
>you'll be stuck in this fuckin'
>
>rat's hole forever."

The C.O. snarls as Quincy continues,

>"Think I'm gonna choose William Fredrick
>
>as my new name...but you can call me Bill...
>
>okay?" he mockingly taunts to the officer.

His cell door swings open and Quincy exits. As he passes the guard, the C.O. whacks Quincy across the shoulder blades,

>"But until then...you're mine
>
>asshole."

Without showing an inch of reactions, Quincy confidently strides to his meeting with destiny.

Chapter 37

-----The crispy snap of Luc slicing some lettuce for their lunchtime

sandwiches draws Philippe's attention away from staring at his phone,

    "Not too much mayo Luc...

    and just a spot of black pepper."

Luc complies with his brother's request,

    "Renee should be calling

    soon...right?"

Philippe nods his head and gestures for Luc to bring their lunch into the

living room. Taking their respective seats,

    "Things are gonna go down

    really fast now Luc...and I

    know the way LeSean's mind

    works. His fuckin' plan is

    eliminating US...then every

    link on the chain leading back

    to him."

    "Link on a chain?"

Philippe pats him on the arm,

"Think about it lil' bro...once

Quincy's history, the only way

LeSean will feel safe, is getting

rid of us too...blow you and me

away...then disappear with ALL

the money."

Luc finishes a bite of his sandwich,

"Holy shit...what the fuck are

we gonna do Philippe?"

Philippe grabs his phone and stares at it for a moment,

"We'll wait for Renee's confirmation

that everything went down as planned...

then I'll know exactly how to

handle LeSean."

Luc continues to chow down his lunchtime snack as his brother stares at

the clock...waiting for his cousin's call.

-----Quincy strolls into the interrogation room, flanked by his attorney,

Dan O'Shea. Derrick, already seated at the interrogation table, scans his

counter-points then immediately decides his course of action. Quincy attempts to make a smart-ass remark, but Derrick's patented psychotic-

stare takes him off-guard and he stammers,

> "Listen Mister Detective...

> I need..."

Derrick slams his briefcase shut,

> "I'll tell you what you need

> Mister White...you're in

> desperate need of my

> mother fuckin' help."

Quincy looks over at O'Shea, hoping for a clever response to Derrick's

remarks. Dan obliges and questions Derrick,

> "We need your help...

> how's that Detective?"

Derrick, still locked onto Quincy's eyes, leans back into his chair,

> "The way my D.A. sees it Mr. Public

> Defender...your client here...

> he played his hand too early

> in the game."

Derrick begins to laugh while talking,

> "Seems that when Tough-Guy

here was first locked-up...

he was babbling like a little bitch...

telling the whole world to hear

about some very bad men."

Derrick slams his fist upon the table,

"Hey dumb-ass...we KNOW

that if we do nothing...no protection...

no relocation...just say fuck-it to your

so-called information...you're a

fuckin' dead man Quincy!"

A severely rattled Quincy yelps towards Dan,

"Dead...what the fuck's he

talking about?"

Derrick opens his briefcase, takes out a file and slides it across the table.

Dan begins to read as Derrick informs Quincy,

"We've already worked it out

with your lawyer's boss...drop

the pot-charges...just let you fly

free as a bird...then right into

the waiting arms of those

scumbags that you were talking

about. We'll just let the

WHOLE WORLD know that you're

cooperating with us fully.

We're pretty damn confident that

you'll see things our way Quincy...

but I guess that's only true if your

plan was to keep-on breathing

past one o'clock today."

Derrick stands as Dan lifts the file to his face and whispers to Quincy.

Derrick walks over to the opposite side of the room as Scott talks into his

ear,

"You got 'em on the ropes Derrick.

They're going to ask for a few

moments alone to discuss their

response...casually grant their

request and we've got a first

round knock-out Derrick."

Right on-cue Dan responds,

"I need a few minutes alone

to confer with my client."

Derrick grins as Scott says,

"K.O."

Derrick nods his head in agreement with Dan's appeal and heads towards

the door to give them the time requested.

-----"Scott said what to you?"

Sophia asks Ellen, about five

minutes into their midday

phone conversation.

Ellen finishes a sip of her coffee,

"I know...right? A weekend

in Connecticut...I couldn't

believe how easy it was saying,

"Of course Scott, I'd love to spend

the weekend with you.

Do you think we're rushing

things Sophia?"

"You're two grown-ups who've been

alone a long time...oops, one second,

Scott just emailed me."

Sophia reads Scott's email then types a response,

 "Great news so far Ellen...

 Scott says Detective Hayes

 is on the verge of a breakthrough.

 This whole nightmare might finally

 be coming to an end."

Ellen takes a moment to contemplate Sophia's remark,

 "From your lips to God's

 ears darling."

-----Ronnie stands at the back of the line entering the prison cafeteria. A loud radio-dispatch from C.O. Carolan's receiver diverts the attention of the other officer who's guarding the door's entrance. With cover from the commotion, Ronnie deftly slips over to a small adjacent hallway then darts down a passage.

 Moments later, he reaches the linen closet Renee had mapped out and slips into the unlocked door. He takes a deep breath in order to recall the remaining instructions...

 ...You're almost home if you'd made

 it this far Menoni. C.O.Tucker is

 around the next bend, he's the

only one guarding the gate.

He's been paid well so smash

that fucker with everything

you've got.

Ronnie, shivering with fear but sweating in anticipation, remembers on...

...Take the key from his belt

and unlock the gate. BEFORE

entering, take the smear of

toothpaste from behind your

ear and reach through the bars...

rub it on the camera's lens

mounted on the corner of

the wall.

Ronnie stands, slowly opens the linen room door and cautiously peeks

out...It's ON!

Chapter 38

-----12:09-----

-----The blurred image of Ronnie darting down the hallway towards
Interrogation Room #2 flashes on the prison's monitor. Carolan's created
a second commotion at the lunchroom that has diverted the attention
away from the attending officer, so Ronnie's dash goes unnoticed.

-----Scott's typing a message to Sophia on his computer while talking into
Derrick's ear,

>"Alright Derrick, slip back in
>
>there and let's wrap this
>
>puppy up."

Derrick points over to Dan and Quincy that's he's going to leave the room
to fill their request,

>"All over it bossman."

He indicates to the attending C.O. to open the interrogation room's door.
The C.O. unlocks the heavy metal door and pulls it open. They both enter
and head towards Quincy.

-----Moments later, Ronnie reaches the same interrogation room door, he
rips away the metal flask that he had earlier taped to his back. But then,
with complete surprise, the door opens in front of him. He fumbles with

the key and it tumbles to the floor. Quickly regaining his composure, Ronnie pulls the stopper off the silver flask and launches the improvised-mortar into Interrogation Room #2.

Without looking back, Ronnie runs back towards the cafeteria...and hopefully his timely escape.

----Ronnie's shiny I.E.D. settles to the floor in the corner of the interrogation room, allowing only a second for any reaction.

The attending C.O. surprisingly pushes Derrick to safety behind the opened door then dives towards the explosive device. In mid-leap, the shrapnel erupts and invades the heroic officer's chest and torso, killing him instantly.

The blast traps Derrick's upper-body between the door and wall, slamming him unconscious as the metal shards bounce throughout the smoke-filled room, saturating Dan and Quincy's bodies. As the four men lay about the floor, Scott's screams go unheard,

"DERRICK....DERRICK!"

Chapter 39

-----12:12-----

-----Frankie glances at the cafeteria's wall clock and realizes it's time for

his scene in Renee's play. Walking with tray in hand back to his normal

lunch table, Frankie purposely trips over a fellow inmates extended leg.

He dramatically tumbles to the ground as his food spills on the floor.

Frankie jumps back to his feet and screams at the duped-inmate,

"What the hell mother-fucker...

you wanna go?"

Frankie flails his arms as the two meet and begin to tussle. The melee

draws the attention of the C.O. guarding the cafeteria doors and he runs

over to the brawl. With perfect timing, this allows Ronnie the opportunity

to sneak through the door and join the cheering crowd.

-----The smoke wafting through the Interrogation Room #2 begins settling

to the ceiling.

Escaping his unconsciousness, Derrick slides the door open that

he's been pinned behind. He surveys the destroyed room, spots Quincy

writhing in pain and drags himself across the floor. Finally reaching the

mortally wounded Quincy, Derrick has yet to notice the substantial blood

trail pumping from his shattered leg. Just as the prison's alarm system begins to wail, Derrick slinks up next to the gasping inmate. With his last

breath, the dying Quincy utters,

> "Three...scumbags...Luc….
>
> Philippe...LeSean..."

Quincy spits up a reddened mix of lung and blood,

> "Get those...mother-fuckers..."

Quincy's eyes close for the last time as Derrick then rolls off him and onto

his back,

> "Derrick...is that you?"
>
> calls over the Bluetooth.
>
> "Yeah...it's me boss."

Derrick violently coughs from the still present smoke. He looks at Quincy's

limp body,

> "Don't think we're getting anything..."

Spitting up blood with his next horrible cough,

> "Outta this asshole...Mr. District...
>
> Attorney..."
>
> "Shhhh Derrick...someone's coming
>
> to help...they'll be right there buddy."

Derrick's eyes blur then he loses consciousness as a group of EMT's come rushing into the smoke-filled room.

Chapter 40

The elevator doors of Memorial General's third-floor ICU Unit open. Ellen exits the lift, swiftly makes her way over to the ICU's waiting-room and spots Sophia watching the nightly local news. She waves to Sophia, rushes to her side and they share a deep embrace,

"How's Detective Hayes doing?

Sounded pretty awful from the

smidgen of info you gave me."

Sophia points at the television mounted on the wall,

"It's all over the news.

C'mon, we'll watch it together."

"Okay…where's Scott? Is he in

with Detective Hayes? You said

he was in contact with Derrick

when it all went down…

what happened?"

Reaching the seats in front of the television,

'Scott's talking to the doctors

right now…and someone killed

the convict they were scheduled

to talk to...Derrick seems to have

got caught up in the crossfire."

They sit next to each other and begin watching Channel 7's veteran

Anchorman report on the story,

"That was Jim Robinson reporting

from the scene of today's brazen

attack. Now to recap the story...

A few minutes after noon today,

a yet to be identified assailant

used an improvised explosive

device to kill three and gravely

wound a high-ranking detective

from the New Jersey State Police."

A photo of Derrick flashes on-screen,

"Detective Derrick Hayes,

shown here, is listed in

grave-condition and is

currently in surgery."

The waiting-room doors slowly open; Scott enters and sees the girls

intently watching the television.

He quietly walks over, takes a seat and Sophia whispers,

"Oh Scott...I can't believe Derrick..."

"He's going to be okay...he just got

out of surgery. The doctor said he's

still in critical, but finally a stable

condition."

Ellen reaches over and grabs Scott's hand,

"Are you okay?"

Their eyes meet and they share a smile as Scott gently squeezes her

dainty fingers,

"Much better now that I've

got my two girls with me."

Their warm moment is interrupted by a breaking-report,

"This just in... Channel 7 has

exclusive video from today's

assault at the Prison."

An unedited video from today's attack plays as the anchorman speaks the

voice-over,

"These scenes are graphic...

please be advised...this

recently obtained video

shows the final moments."

The replay of Derrick and Quincy's last moments together shakes them all

to the core. The anchorman continues,

"It appears that the wounded

Detective Hayes shares a final

conversation with the deceased

convict...who I'm being told is

Quincy White, a local narcotics

dealer."

Upon hearing the news an enraged Scott barks out,

"Unbelievable!"

Sophia and Scott pull out their cellphones and flip their switches to full

battle-mode. Sophia responds to Scott's question before he asks it,

"I'll have the Governor's office

on the line in a moment."

He acknowledges Sophia's remark then yells into his cellphone,

"I want answers right now...

I need to know from Channel 7

how raw video from an on-going

investigation and CRIME SCENE

gets splashed on T.V. for the

whole world to see."

Sophia taps Scott's shoulder,

"I have the Governor holding."

Sophia hands her phone to Scott, he mouths the words "thank you" then

begins talking to the Governor,

"Good evening Mr. Governor."

Scott pauses, noticing that a visibly shaken Ellen is staring into the

distance,

"Just one moment sir...

something's just come to

my attention."

Scott sets the cellphone down and gently caresses Ellen's arm. She comes

out of her daze as he takes his large hand and cups her face with it. Their

lips draw close and they share a quick kiss. As their eyes reopen, Scott

whispers,

"I'm gonna make this right Ellen...

rest assured...I'm on it."

Scott slips in one more peck then restarts his phone conversation. Sophia

then puts her arm around Ellen's shoulder,

> "Scott will take care of this whole

> mess...no doubt about it."

> "I can see that...the Big Guy's got it all handled."

Sophia gestures for them to take a seat,

> "Let's see what else the news has to say."

Ellen nods her head in agreement as they return to the television.

Chapter 41

The Channel 7 News report has Luc glued to his big-screen T.V...he's following the details of today's happenings at the Prison as Philippe and LeSean talk over his speakerphone.

"LeSean...I'm watching Quincy

whisper something to that

detective right now."

LeSean pauses to take-in the new information,

"Listen Philippe...this is some

serious shit here. We need to

dump our bullshit quarrels...

get it back to how it used to be...

like back when we first started

all this fun...you down?"

Philippe thinks for a moment,

"Sounds good LeSean...so what

you thinking's the best way to handle

that cop?"

"My mind's been racing since I got

the news from Renee...then seeing

this shit on T.V."

Luc chimes in,

>"It's simple...what we need to do is
>
>bide our time. Sounds like that
>
>Detective's probably not gonna
>
>make it anyway, and if he's dead,
>
>then the info dies with him."

Luc eases back into the couch and relishes his insight. LeSean quickly adds,

>"If he makes it...I see someone
>
>slipping into his hospital room one
>
>night, silencing him permanently."

Philippe shakes his head in agreement,

>"Okay then...we'll meet up once
>
>we see what happens with that
>
>fuckin' pig. When you in town LeSean?"
>
>"Saturday late...maybe Sunday. I'll blow
>
>by your place when I get back."

Philippe reconsiders,

>"Make it Sunday at five...

everything should be played

out by then and we'll know

how best to move."

"Done...I'll be there."

Luc, now looking quite relieved, turns to his brother as the phone goes

dead,

"So...we all good now with LeSean?"

"Fuck that piece of shit. I wouldn't

trust him as far as I could throw his

fuckin' afro-American ass."

"So what then Philippe?"

Philippe shakes his head and grins,

"We're takin' your advice lil' bro...

we're gonna wait and see how

this game all plays out.

Then, and only then am I gonna

gut that mother fucker LeSean."

They ease into their couch and continue following the news coverage.

Chapter 42

The utter stillness of the Prison-on-lockdown has Ronnie's nerves

on the brink as he fidgets on his cot. The day's maniacal events replay

over and over in his head and he stares blankly ahead,

"Did everything go as planned?

Will my sweet Jasmine ever get

to see her next birthday? Did I

really just take someone's life?

Oh sweet Jesus...what have I done?"

His internal conflict is interrupted by the far-off closing of a door, followed

by the steady clicking of a Corrections Officer's heals against the corridor's

tiled floor. His heart begins to race as the tap-tap-tap gets louder and

louder,

"This is it...this is it, I just know it."

Ronnie begins to hyperventilate as the rhythmic gate of the C.O.'s stride

halts directly in front of his barred door. The unidentified C.O. says in a

muted voice,

"You almost made it Menoni.

Renee had it all set up for you...

follow the plan and nothing

happens to your daughter."

Ronnie nervously asks the unidentified voice,

> "What did I miss? I followed
>
> his instructions to the letter."

The C.O. retorts,

> "Shut up you piece of shit.
>
> They found the fucking key
>
> you dropped asshole."

Ronnie remembers the interrogation door opening in front of him and then his faux pas comes to light...He sees the key dropping and clanging on the ground.

> "For little Jasmine's sake...you'd better
>
> pray that nothing comes back to you
>
> from their investigation. Just one link...
>
> and your whole family's gonna be
>
> renamed the Missing-Links."

The C.O. starts to walk away but can't resist one parting shot,

> "Get some rest Menoni...you're gonna need it."

Chapter 43

A light tapping at the Crime Unit's Video-Analysis room door grabs

the attention of Dr. Paul. He's been dissecting yesterday's hacked-video

since six this morning,

"Door's open."

Scott strides into the darkened room, sees Dr. Paul fixated on a video-

monitor and with a fatherly tone asks,

"How are you holding up Paul?

Sorry I missed you at the hospital

last night..."

Scott scans the monitors and angrily spouts,

"...but that damn video took up

my whole night."

Paul turns from the monitors,

"Just wished I could have been

here sooner...my plane from

D.C. didn't land until after midnight."

Paul wipes the moistness from his eyes and tries to speak, but just can't

find the words. Scott puts his arm around Paul's shoulder,

"He's a tough-nut Paulie...

If anyone's gonna pull through...

it's Derrick. You've known him

since what, you were both six

years old? With that foster-family

back in the ninety's, right?

Have you EVER seen him give up...

even once?"

Paul shakes his head no and accepts Scott's council,

"I've been working on the hacked-

video all morning Scott.

Plus I got the video from the outside

corridor, near the Interrogation Room...

someone knew what they were doing...

barely anything usable."

Paul types on his keyboard,

"I'm operating with NASA on this cutting

edge nano-pixel technology...

I'm running his video through the

program right now. It's just the

video quality is incredibly poor

after the explosion...I just have

to find the right tweak to this

program."

Comfortingly patting Paul on the arm,

"I know you will Paul...but remember,

Derrick's going to wake up soon and

tell us what he knows...all by himself."

"I know you're right...he is one damn

tough coconut."

Scott winks then stands to leave. Paul enters a few more bits of info into

his computer program,

"I know what's on my plate...

what on deck for you Mr. D.A.?"

"A very serious day...of getting to

the bottom of god-damned things.

I've had it up to here with all this

going through the proper channels...

I'm grabbin' this bull by his big hairy

balls and taking him right to

the ground."

Reaching out and grabbing Scott for a handshake,

"Well then don't let me get in your

way Big Guy...go make it happen."

Chapter 44

The whistle of a teapot beckons loudly for a response. Sophia

rushes into her kitchen, turns off the burner then pours hot water into her

preset cup. After grabbing a lemon wedge, she notices the V.A. Calendar

hanging on the cork board next to her fridge.

Tacked-up next to the calendar is an old family photo of her late

husband Chauncey and their two girls, Stephanie and Jenny. Sophia

touches the faded image of a youthful Chauncey,

"My sweet...has it really been

twelve years since I last kissed you?"

She looks again at the photo,

"It's funny the way people are wired

Chauncey. I can remember the day

you died, June 8th, like it was

yesterday...but the following ninth

or tenth? I couldn't tell you if I

even breathed those days.

Sophia notices today's Friday April 8th on her calendar,

"Chauncey...I don't know how much

more of this high-stakes, life and death

pressure that I can handle. This week

has been a blur to me my love."

Sophia glances at the photo and smiles at the silly face her Jenny made,

on the beach that beautiful summer day.

She laughs that Jenny grew-up to be the true mother-hen of their little

group,

"What would you say to all of my

bellyaching Jenny-poo."

Sophia stands-up and imitates her tightly wound daughter,

"You'll stop someday Mommy...

the day Hell freezes-over and you

feel like you're not being an

important cog in the grand wheels

of Justice!"

After blowing them each a kiss, she notices that there's a tapping at her

back door,

"Coming...one moment please."

Scurrying out of her chair, she then twists open the doorknob. To Sophia's

surprise, there stands Ellen, looking like she's about to burst with

happiness. Sophia grabs her hand and gently tugs Ellen inside,

"Well c'mon in here Little Miss Sunshine."

Sophia scans Ellen's appearance then jokes,

"Looks like somebody didn't make it

home last night...hmmm...I wonder

who that could be?"

She bounces past Sophia, goes to the cabinet and pulls out a teacup and saucer. Sophia smiles at Ellen's complete familiarity with her home,

"Looks like Miss Matchmaker

here hit the nail on the

head, huh?"

Ellen finishes making her tea,

"If I were a dandelion Sophia...

my head would pop-off with

excitement."

They take their seats at the nook as Sophia prods her for info. She already knows that Scott had contacted Ellen late last night...and that they had a bite to eat at the Mark Twain afterwards. But what could have brought this fairy princess...with a smile the size of Texas...to her kitchen this morning all disheveled?

"Okay...what's up?"

Ellen's eyes sparkle as she regales,

> "What do you want first?
>
> The great news, the REALLY
>
> great news…or the just so crazy,
>
> I couldn't handle it all by myself
>
> Great News?"

Sophia sits back and readies for the incoming goodies,

> "Okay Ellen…the great news first."
>
> "Perfect…just like I had rehearsed it…
>
> on my way over…from Scott's house."

Sophia cheers,

> "That's fantastic…it's funny how
>
> people can work so close together…
>
> but never see each other in that
>
> CERTAIN way…that is until a
>
> lightning bolt strikes."

Ellen smirks,

> "Or until our dear friend Sophia
>
> sets up a lightning rod during a
>
> thunderstorm in your backyard."

Sharing a laugh Ellen then remarks,

"It's crazy you said lightning striking...

right after we first kissed the other

night...that's what I saw...lightning."

Sophia does a sexy Mae West impersonation,

"I know about the lightning...

but howz about the THUNDER baby?"

Without thinking Ellen grabs the table, shakes it and belts-out,

"KABOOOOOM!"

After sharing another laugh, they finally regain some composure as Ellen

continues,

"Seriously...I hope you know that

you don't EVER have to worry about

me getting between you and Scott...

he adores you Sophia. He told me

that if it wasn't for you...after losing

Sarah...there was absolutely no way

that he'd be where he is today...

and he definitely wouldn't be half

the man without you in his life."

Sophia is deeply affected by the confirmation that all her years of dedicated service has really mattered. Ellen starts with her Really Great news,

> "Now the really great news...
>
> Detective Hayes is being released
>
> from the I.C.U. ward later today."

Sophia breathes a sigh of relief,

> "Now, he's still in a coma and not
>
> out of the woods yet...but Scott
>
> said the prognosis was definitely
>
> a positive one."
>
> "That Derrick is something special
>
> Ellen...he's poured every ounce of
>
> himself into finding some justice
>
> for you...and catching those sons
>
> of bitches."

Reaching into her handbag Ellen then nervously pulls out an envelope with some odd looking postage,

> "Sophia...The reason I look like this...
>
> like I did the walk of shame over to

your place...I went home after Scott's

and grabbed yesterday's mail."

She holds up the envelope,

"I got another letter from Tommy."

Sophia's jaw drops as Ellen places the letter on the table,

"I didn't know what to do Sophia...

I knew it was from him...

that handwriting is an easy

giveaway. I couldn't even open it...

my hands started trembling

when I tried to."

Sophia reaches across the table then places her hands around Ellen's,

"We'll find out honey...together."

Sophia picks up the envelope, opens it then carefully unfurls Tommy's

letter. Placing it on the tabletop they then begin to read,

Mom,

I've enlisted our friend Sophia,

my dear Lil' Miss Worry Wort.

In order to keep a certain secret

cloaked from your view.

Not sure exactly why I asked

my buddy Xavier to send this

letter addressed from England...

just thought it'd be funny

getting a clue from abroad

and maybe throw you off the track

never materialized but I went with

it anyway Mommy...I LOVE YOU!!

You're the only one who's ever

understood my weird sense of humor.

Ellen breaks down in tears upon reading Tommy's sentiment. She weeps

uncontrollably as Sophia darts around the nook to console her. As they

hug, Ellen cries out,

"MY SWEET, SWEET BABY...

OHHHHHHH!"

Ellen grabs even tighter as Sophia strokes her back,

"I know darlin'...I know."

Ellen releases their embrace then wipes her eyes,

"I raised such a great kid."

"The best Ellen...Tommy's the absolute best."

Sophia wipes a tear from Ellen's face then points to the letter,

"Let's get back to Tommy's letter...

I need to know what he's up to.

You KNOW I would've been his

main minion...I wonder, once

he told me what the secret was,

if I could have kept it from you?"

Sophia bends to sit and scooches Ellen to one side of the chair. Sophia

picks up the letter and they continue reading,

Okay Mommy...if all has gone as

scheduled, you have nary a clue of

the life-changing event that may

lie just a month before you.

There are some serious pratfalls

leading up to May and the outcome

still hangs perilously in the balance.

Therein lies the true reason for this

whole smoke and mirrors game.

I realize that since I went away

to school, we haven't been able

to talk every day, like the old times,

but please know that you'll always

be my best girl! But......?

That's it doll...now please don't

go trying to pry Sophia for any info...

she'll have been SWORN to secrecy.

One Final Letter, with the true grace

of God, will cross your mailbox putting

the missing puzzle pieces of our lives

together.

Always Yours,

Sam

The girls sit motionless for nearly a minute, shell shocked by Tommy's

letter. Sophia then breaks the silence,

"Sam...what's with Tommy

signing Sam?"

Ellen hears Sophia's query, comes out of her trance and begrudgingly

chuckles,

"My boy...even when I'm at my lowest,

Tommy could always make me laugh.

I haven't called him Sam since he was

in Little-League...he used it as our

private nickname for him."

Sophia stands and walks to the refrigerator as Ellen continues,

"I used to embarrass the hell out of

Tommy at his baseball games.

He begged me not to yell so loud,

but I just couldn't stop doing it."

Opening the refrigerator door, Sophia jokingly says,

"Oh...I can definitely see that happening.

If another little boy slid into him hard or

threw a ball at Tommy...you'd probably

run on the field and go spank 'em."

"He even asked me not to come anymore,

but then we came to a mutual agreement.

I could still come see him play, but ONLY

if I'd yell-out the name Sam...so he'd be

the only one to know who that crazy

lady in the bleachers was yelling for."

Sophia places a small plate with two mini-chocolate éclairs on the nook's table then takes her seat,

>"That's gotta be the cutest story
>
>I've ever heard...where'd he get
>
>Sam from?"

Ellen shrugs her shoulders then notices the clock on the wall has already rounded seven-thirty,

>"Sweetie...I know you've got a
>
>busy Friday ahead."

Sophia nods her head in reluctant agreement,

>"And I have my therapy session tonight...
>
>meet up at the Twain afterwards?"
>
>"Perfect...we'll go over all the day's
>
>happenings then we'll tackle Tommy's
>
>letter. Plus, we'll get Scott to help us."

They pick-up an éclair, tap their pastries together then toast to the interesting Friday that lies ahead.

Chapter 45

The Prison's "High-Alert" status is still in effect as three C.O.

guards intently look for a missing inmate.

"Where the fuck is he Carolan?"

barks Senior C.O. Billings.

C.O. Carolan shrugs his shoulders,

"How the hell should I know Cap?

He couldn't have just disappeared."

Billings scratches his head then barks out their next move,

"Alright...Diaz, take the point down

to the access stairwell...Carolan

and I will swing-up around the flank...

that should cover our bases down here."

They each go in search of Ronnie as Billings calls out,

"C'mon Menoni...the jig is up buddy.

Turn yourself in...I'm sure there are

extenuating circumstances to why

you killed C.O. Jenkins and that

Public Defender."

He rounds another corner of the laundry room as Diaz calls-out loudly,

"Cappy, you need to get over

here...pronto!"

Billings and Carolan hear the distress call, dart towards the stairwell then

see Diaz staring at something at the bottom of the stairs,

"Oh shit" Billings says upon reaching

Diaz's position.

Carolan's spots Ronnie's limp mass lying next to the stairs,

"Guess Menoni's fingerprints on that

key doesn't mean a damn thing now."

Billings shoots Carolan a dirty look then speaks into his walkie-talkie,

"Base...this is Billings. We have an

incident down here in the laundry

room. Menoni is dead, looks like this

piece of shit tripped and fell down the stairwell."

Billings sternly looks at his counterparts. They nod their heads in

agreement with his assessment of the situation.

"Get Medical down here...to the

Laundry's back stairway."

Billings wipes his brow as Carolan quietly snorts to himself,

"Renee's gonna to be pleased with my handy work."

Chapter 46

The steady beep-beep of the heart monitor reassures Dr. Paul

that his buddy is going to pull through this ordeal. Derrick, covered mostly

in gauze, lies recuperating as Paul stares at the photos he placed near D's

bedside. Tommy Carpenter's smiling face, the Weinstein's celebrating an

anniversary, Sally Tighes parasailing in the Caribbean...all from Derrick's

wallet. Scott walks in,

"How's our boy doing Paul?"

Scott takes a seat on the opposite side of the bed as Paul points to the

machines monitoring Derrick's fragile condition,

"Better, but he lost a ton of blood Scott.

Everything's looking good, but they really

have no idea how long this coma could last...

could be tomorrow or months from now."

Scott notices Derrick's photographs and picks-up the one picture lying

face down...he knows who these two teenagers are. Turning the

photograph around for Paul to see,

"I wonder who these two

knuckleheads are."

Paul laughs remembering the trip

up to Lake George with their

foster-family, the Wagner's.

"You know this crazy son of

a bitch saved my life that day."

Scott hands him the photo,

"It was about an hour after this

snapshot was taken."

Paul places the photo back on the table,

"We were swimming pretty far out

on the lake when Patrick, the oldest

of Grammy Wagner's grandsons,

"accidentally" rowed up in his

Canoe and smashed me with an

oar. Son of a bitch left me out

there for dead. Lucky Derrick was

diving underwater at the time…

Patrick never saw him."

Paul moves his curly brown hair near his temple for Scott to see,

"Check this out…I still have the scar.

Holy shit, I was bleeding like a

stuffed pig out there on the water.

This marvelous son of a bitch

swam us both back to shore...

over a quarter mile."

Paul takes a seat next to Derrick and places his hand upon Paul's shoulder,

"Now you're here for him Paulie...

that's what brothers do for each other...

always have each other's back."

"Thanks man...and just to let you

know, I have made some progress

with the video, so I'll keep you posted."

Scott taps Derrick's arm,

"That's great. We're releasing some

info to the public today...

hoping someone in the community

will step up and give us some assistance."

"You're still running into a brick wall?"

"Info's coming in dribs and drabs...

I'm going full-court pressure starting

today. Gonna turn the heat up and

nab these assholes before anyone

else gets hurt."

After sharing a "high-five", they both take a seat and attentively gaze at

their recuperating friend.

Chapter 47

Scrolling down the Channel 7 News Internet page, Luc comes across a NEWS-FLASH-Video that hits too close to home,

--- A Channel 7 EXCLUSIVE---

---Good News Follow-Up Story---

"This reporter is thrilled to report

breaking news...Detective Derrick

Hayes has been released from the

I.C.U Unit of Memorial Hospital

and his prognosis is good.

Additionally, there have been

leaks of a major break in the case

Detective Hayes was working on..."

Upon hearing this dire news, Luc begins to hyperventilate,

"I gotta call Philippe. He'll know

exactly what to do."

Grabbing his phone, Luc begins to dial his brother's number...then abruptly stops,

"Damn...he's unreachable...

in Philly til' tomorrow night...

SHIT!"

Luc paces nervously then comes to a conclusion,

"LeSean...he'll know what to do...

maybe just killin' that cop is the

right call."

He taps LeSean's contact-number and seconds later, a voice asks,

"What's up lil' man Luc?"

Luc nervously stammers,

"I'm freakin' out LeSean...that cop

is recovering and 5-0's got some info

on us...we're fucked man."

After a brief moment of silence, LeSean confidently replies,

"Relax little man...where's Philippe?"

"That's just it...he's in Philly doing

that thing...and can't be reached."

"Shit, that's right. Wait, I've got it...

your Grannie used to work at

Memorial as an orderly, right?"

"Yeah, I think it was Memorial...so..."

LeSean sternly answers,

"Just think man...it was your plan, right?

Killing that piece of shit pig...just ask

Grannie if she can remember a secret

way in-and-out of Memorial. You know

how to jog her memory the best Luc.

And then slice that mother-fucker's

throat wide open...so he can't talk."

There's a dead silence until LeSean barks out,

"The balls in your court Luc...

you're the only one who can

save our asses my brother...

STEP UP!"

Luc again starts to pace. He's unsure if he's got what it takes to complete

the task. He pounds his fist upon the table,

"I'll do it right LeSean...

gonna slice that Pig up like a

Haitian mountain-boar."

"That's right lil' man Luc...

go make it happen."

Luc hangs up the phone then darts up the stairs to talk to Grannie.

Chapter 48

Watching the news over the last week has Alexis quite excited.

Believing an arrest for her parent's murder maybe soon be at hands, she's

begun the next phase of her strategy. All that's needed for its

implementation is a positive response from the Prison Board.

Patiently waiting for the evening's mail delivery, she nearly jumps

out of her chair when the mailman slides her parcels through the front

door's slot. Nearly catching the mail before it hits the floor, she then darts

back to her desk and tears into the N.Y. Department of Corrections letter,

Dear Ms. Weinstein,

The loving sentiment of your

application to enroll in our Charity

Outreach Program has touched my

heart. It's with sincere appreciation

and happiness to inform you that

your application has been accepted.

I will be meeting with you personally

at the prison Welcome Center.

We'll go over all your first day's

itinerary then. God Bless you Alexis

and thank you again for your

substantial donation.

Yours Truly,

Dr. Gayle Andrews

Folding the letter neatly, Alexis puts it to the side on her desk, then

notates the $125,000.00 Donation Check in her bank statement. After

entering the amount, she taps the pen to her chin,

"A small price to pay for some needed

retribution. Plus...ya can't take it with

ya now can ya?"

Alexis' mind begins to spin with her end-game's payoff. Noticing the time

in the corner of her computer, her demeanor does a one-eighty,

"Time for Ellen and Dr. Alton...better

get moving."

Grabbing her car keys, she rearranges her paperwork then shuffles off to

this Friday session.

Chapter 49

Reclined in his familiar posture, Renee lies comfortably on his cot just finishing his copy of Crime and Punishment. Engrossed in the Russian tale's climax, Carolan's appearance barely goes noticed as he whispers over to Renee,

"Pssst...Renee, it's all handled.

I took care of Menoni, just like

you asked."

Renee spins off the cot, grabs a few baggies from underneath his bed then slowly walks over to him. Reaching through the bars and yanking Carolan close, he jams the bags into his shirt pocket,

"Remember asshole...Julie and your precious

little Mark are counting on your continued

cooperation. Enjoy your smack jerk-off."

Renee releases Carolan from his grasp as the C.O. stutters a response,

"You got it...no problems here...

just tell me where and when Renee...

I'm always your guy."

Renee grimaces while wiping his hands clean on Carolan's shirt,

"Good...job well done. Looks like your

little family's gonna make it after all

Carolan."

Carolan dashes away as Renee returns to his cot and back to his literary

escape.

Chapter 50

Sharon the waitress winks at Ellen as she places tonight's special,

a plate of open-faced roast beef with mashed potatoes, in front of her.

Sharon asks Sophia,

"Lil' more coffee?"

Sophia flashes an I'm okay-sign,

"Mmmm...that looks good Ellen.

My salad's looking pretty lame."

They share a smile as Sophia sprinkles some parmesan cheese on top of

her salad in a futile attempt to give her greens some pep,

"So, sounds like you and Alexis

are really getting close, huh?"

After sampling a bite of her roast beef,

"You have no idea. The way we

opened up to each other this session,

about our shared grief, makes me feel

like I'm making real progress...then

learning of our mutual connection to

the crimes. I can't believe the

coincidence...two people, struggling

to survive, meet at a court ordered

doctor's appointment then wind up

trying to save each other from all

of the madness."

Ellen shakes her head,

"The look on her face Sophia...

when we started comparing

notes. I mentioned that

Detective Hayes was attacked...

we realized that my Det. Hayes

was her Det. Hayes and that her

parents were killed by the same

animals that took my Tommy...

she seemed relieved. Like,

she wasn't alone in the world."

Sophia chokes-up thinking of Derrick,

"Scott said that Derrick had

Tommy's and the Weinstein's

pictures in his wallet. They're

like his family. God,I love that guy."

Ellen smiles at the notion of Derrick caring for Tommy like family.

Recalling her session,

"I don't know what it is about
Dr. Alton's office...I just feel so
safe there. I'm figuring out so
many things that I didn't realize
were tormenting me. I know it's
only been two meetings...

...but I feel like I'm healing."

Sophia grins as Ellen continues,

"But poor Alexis...she's really so
amazing. She's got stage three
brain-cancer, lost the only family
that she had, and somehow has
decided to serve prisoners food
over in New York for charity."

Sophia puts down her fork,

"Wow...what a strong girl."

Ellen agrees but says with a puzzled look,

"There's something though...

deeper...or darker about her.

I can tell that Dr. Alton has some

reservations about Alexis working

at that prison...I overheard him asking

Mrs. Duvall to schedule a call with

someone with the New York's prison

system...he sounded very concerned."

Ellen disregards her intuitions,

"I'm sure it's nothing...she seemed so

happy and talkative by the time we

were done our session."

Ellen prepares for another bite then quickly states,

"Oh yeah...Alexis and I are planning

to go see Detective Hayes early

tomorrow morning. Want to join us?"

Sophia shakes her head side to side,

"Sorry, Scott's got me booked up

all morning. I'm going to see

Derrick tomorrow night."

Sophia remembers another thought,

"Oh, I forgot to mention something great. Scott linked me up with Dr. Paul Carol...a great buddy of Derrick's. I've known him forever too. He does these computer simulations... the Big Guy thinks if you tell Paul about Tommy and the two letters that he sent us, he just might be able to crack Tommy's code."

With excitement Ellen says,

"That's terrific Sophia...it's all coming together. I've saved most of Tommy's riddles and puzzles that he created for me over the years. That should give the good doctor a big head start."

Sophia nods in agreement,

"Definitely sweetie. Plus, I've already booked reservations for you two lovebirds at Umberto's over in Little Italy for tomorrow night."

Ellen taps Sophia on the hand,

"You are simply the best Sophia."

Sophia strokes her hair and jokingly states,

"I know."

Chapter 51

Walking from his Camry and down his apartment's driveway, Philippe has a bounce in his step this cloudless Saturday morning. He's come home earlier than planned to tell Luc of their very good fortunes. He reaches, then swings open the basement door,

"Brother Luc...got some glorious news

little man."

His excitement stems from the fact that they've received more than double the price on their year long haul. After closing the door Philippe bolts over to Luc's bedroom, only to find it unoccupied.

"Well what'd ya know...

lil' man Luc up before the

crack-of-noon on a Saturday."

Philippe's good humor turns when he notices a letter sitting atop the kitchen counter. He walks over, picks up the hand-written letter and begins to read,

Philippe,

If you are reading this note, you musta

came home early from Philly or

something has gone wrong with my plan.

Either way bro, it was the only move I

could make...so don't go freaking on

LeSean if something happens to me...

it was my idea to silence that pig for

good. Grannie told me the layout of

Memorial and by noon it should all be

over and on the news. If not...

just know that I love ya Philippe.

Luc

In a near panic for his brother's welfare, Philippe bounds up the

connecting stairwell to Grannie's. He flies into her apartment,

"Grannie...when did Luc leave?"

Seated in her brown leather Lazy-Boy, Grannie tries to remember exactly

when Luc had left the house.

Philippe paces back and forth, trying to be patient,

"Please Dearie...it's important."

She snaps her fingers,

"I know...QVC came on at eight-thirty

and he left right after that."

Philippe reaches down to kiss Grannie,

"Thank you love...gotta run."

He squeezes her then darts down the stairs,

"I'm gonna kill LeSean if even one

hair on me bro's head is outta place."

After grabbing what he needs from the basement apartment, Philippe

runs to his car then speeds off to Memorial Hospital.

Chapter 52

Standing alone on the hospital elevator, Alexis hums to the background music. The doors slide open and she's pleasantly surprised to see Ellen standing at the nurse's-station waiting for her. Ellen tilts her head and smiles,

"Alexis honey...I am so glad to see you."

They embrace.

-----Knowing that you don't have to be all alone with your grief, especially sharing it with someone whose mutual losses are so interconnected, has morphed two virtual strangers into fast-fallen-sisters.-----

Walking together down the corridor, Alexis reaches out and grabs Ellen's hand. Ellen smiles broadly as they complete the final stretch to Room 312, hand-in-hand. Reaching the Police Officer who's been guarding Derrick's corridor, he checks their Visitor's Passes then they continue the last thirty feet to Derrick's room.

Alexis stops Ellen before they enter,

"Ellen, I know I'm probably gonna cry

when I see Detective Hayes' photos

of my Mom and Dad next to Tommy's...

so hold on tight...and be ready for

some waterworks."

Ellen smiles as she pulls open the door...

...Just a few moments earlier, while shimmying down a drainpipe

from the fourth floor, Luc gingerly attempts to find some footing on the

third floor's ledge. He's devised a plan to sneak-in through the window,

silence Derrick for good then off to the cheers of Philippe and Cousin

Renee.

Slinking across the foot-wide railing, Luc carefully manages the

last five or six feet over to Room 312's partly ajar window. Quietly sliding

the window open the remainder of the way, he then delicately pulls

himself through the narrow opening and sits upon its' ledge.

Reaching into his back pocket, he pulls out a straight-edged razor

and removes the blade's plastic safety. He's primed and ready to

complete his murderous deed...

..."Ahhhhhhhh" screams Alexis as she

walks-in on Luc's treacherous plan.

Her terrifying screams completely unnerve Luc...he scrambles to find a

footing on the ledge for an escape out of the window. Ellen sees his fumbling and inexplicably charges past Derrick's bed then grabs Luc by the legs,

"Let go of me you crazy fuckin'

bitch" he shouts.

Luc contorts himself, twisting back and forth, as Ellen holds on for dear life,

"Never...you're gonna tell me why!"

She flails about as he tries in vain to escape,

"Why did you kill my baby?"

Luc finally breaks free of her grasp and kicks Ellen square in the chest...sending her crashing down to the hospital room floor. The police guard finally reaches Derrick's room, bursts through the door and points his weapon directly at Luc's head,

"Freeze mother-fucker!"

The sight of the officer's gun barrel causes Luc to tense-up for a split second...just enough time to lose the only pressure his hands had upon the window sill.

Amongst all the chaos of the room, Alexis calmly stands and intently watches Luc's reaction to his certain death. Their eyes make direct contact and without hesitation, Alexis grins ear to ear. She then puts her hand up to her face and whimsically, with the tips of her fingers, waves goodbye to him.

Luc's footing finally gives-way and he plummet's the thirty-foot drop onto a picnic table. Alexis rushes over to Ellen, who's now sprawled on the floor,

"Ellen...Ellen can you hear me?"

Writhing in agony, Ellen tries to catch her breath as Alexis scoots behind her head,

"Just lay there sweetie...

someone will be right here...

it's gonna be alright."

Alexis tends to Ellen as the police officer leans out of the window. He spots Luc's lifeless body sprawled amongst the splintered wooden table...a large piece of wood has torn through his chest. Turning from the grisly sight below, he spots the medical team barging into the room. Barking into his chest-mounted microphone,

"I need back-up at Memorial

General...room 312...NOW!"

Chapter 53

Three police cars race by Philippe's Camry as he drives to the hospital. The suspense of whether their flashing lights indicate the fulfillment of Luc's task or that of his brother's capture, steadily madden him. His mind is afire with a thousand different scenarios...most of them running terribly afoul for Luc.

Clenching his hands around the steering wheel, he begins to mumble,

"One hair on Luc's head and you're

dead LeSean...send a boy to do a

man's job will ya?"

Philippe reaches the hospital's roadside entryway, but decides to park in a small strip mall down the street. If something has gone wrong, there's no sense driving right into the lion's den. After parking and a brief walk to the edge of the hospital's perimeter, Philippe spots a Ch7 News camera-crew.

There's a sizable crowd that has formed near the front doors of the hospital. Nonchalantly walking through the maze of cars, Philippe makes his way to the back of the crowd. After a moment or two of attempting to get a snippet of news, he asks a nearby elderly gentleman,

"So Pops, what going down here?"

The senior turns to him,

> "Going down here? What are you talking
>
> about? My wife Gloria is in for a gall stone
>
> removal, imagine that, one stone the size
>
> of her WHOLE gall bladder."
>
> "No old-timer...I mean with all
>
> of this commotion."

The gray-haired gent stammers but then slaps his knee,

> "Oh, I see...you wanna know what's
>
> shakin' bacon....right?"
>
> "Right Pops...so...what's shakin'?"
>
> "Well...seems that some young Haitian
>
> fellow fell out a third story window
>
> and died..."

-----With the words "some young Haitian" and "died"...the world stopped

revolving for Philippe-----

The sweet memories of their youths in Port Au' Prince...frolicking

through the mountainous terrain at their Uncle Pierre's summer home.

Just two young brothers without a care in the world...but all those

beautiful recollections have just crashed and burned. But that brief second of mourning, it is all Philippe will avail himself...he has bigger fish

to fry.

"There's nothing I can do for you

now dear Luc...but vengeance is

mine sayeth the Lord."

In a zombie-like trance, he walks through the parking lot and back over to

his Camry...muttering with every step,

"Sunday with LeSean...

Sunday with LeSean..."

Chapter 54

A female Intern has just finished applying Ellen's chest-wrap as Scott creeps through the examination door. Sophia rises from the chair next to Ellen's bed, walks over to Scott and hugs him. She whispers into his ear,

"This is getting crazy Big Guy?"

He places his hands around her dainty shoulders,

"I've got this handled Sophia.

It's all set for you two to head-up

to Connecticut. I sent all of the

arrangements to your email."

He approaches Ellen and frowns when he sees her grimacing while attempting to slide on her blouse. He asks the doctor,

"How's she doing Doc?"

The young physician makes a notation in Ellen's chart,

"We've got a very lucky lady here,

only two deep abrasions and a slight

tear in her Intercostal space, between

right ribs nine and ten."

Ellen states,

"Enough about me...how's Alexis?

He answers,

 "She's fine...finished with the Detective's

 questioning about an hour ago...I had a

 patrolman take her home."

She tries making light of the situation,

 "Thank you...sweetheart."

Tilting her head to the side,

 "Guess we won't be doing

 dinner at Umberto's in the City

 tonight, huh?"

Scott chuckles as the doctor taps her pen on the chart and states to the

trio,

 "I recommend at least one week

 of R-and-R and she'll be as good

 as new."

Scott confidently states,

 "I've got that all covered Doc."

He looks at Sophia, who's reading his email on her phone,

 "Sophia's got the details all

arranged."

Sophia finishes reading Scott's email,

> "Got that right boss. We're heading
>
> up to Scott's Connecticut house...
>
> and away from this insanity."

The Intern finishes entering the information on Ellen's chart,

> "Well good then, and best of luck
>
> to you Ms. Carpenter...looks like
>
> you're in more than capable hands."

She leaves the examination room as Scott turns to Ellen. He lovingly scolds her,

> "Now young lady...I know you like
>
> excitement, but could we please
>
> refrain from tackling any more
>
> of my murder suspects."

Scott gently touches her face,

> "What were you thinking?

Shrugging her shoulders,

> "When I saw him in the window
>
> trying to escape, all I could think

of was to run and grab him."

Scott hugs her then commandingly says,

>"Like I said...I've got this all handled.
>
>You and Sophia are going up to
>
>Connecticut and I'll be up there
>
>right behind you girls...once
>
>I've figured out the end-game."

Ellen carefully hops off of the exam-table and the three of them head

towards the door. With Ellen in the lead, Sophia leans back, points at Ellen

and silently mouths the words to Scott,

>"Don't worry..."

She touches Ellen's shoulder,

>"...I've got this."

Chapter 55

Alexis sits alone at her desk crisply tapping away on her computer keyboard. Today's crazy events have exasperated the nasty twitch she's been battling since childhood. All of the positive energy from yesterday's session with Dr. Alton has flown right out the window...along with Luc.

Her eyes stare into the computer screen, surfing the net at lightning speed. They widen with excitement...Alexis has just found the nefarious information that she's been looking for,

"Thallium Nitrate...that will handle

all of my needs quite nicely."

Her shoulders suddenly tighten as a violent tic contorts the right side of her face. Alexis grabs a framed photo of her parents,

"Oh Mommy...how I miss you stroking

my hair...telling me it'll be all better."

Another set of facial spasms sends her into a contorted-fit of sobbing. Clenching the picture close to her chest, she searches for an answer to why this happening to her,

"Oh...the pain daddy...I need you!

Please God...help me."

Reaching into one of the desk drawers, she pulls out a large black scarf then places it over her head,

"I remember Mommy...

close my eyes and cover my head...

it'll all be better when I wake up."

Moments later, with the true grace of God, Alexis rests her head on the desk and falls asleep.

Chapter 56

At that same moment and also tapping away on a keyboard, Dr. Paul furiously enters data into his bank of computers. After finishing a long series of algorithms, he runs a computer simulation,

"NON-COMPLIANT ENCRYPTION"

flashes across his many terminals,

Paul throws his clipboard across the room,

"It's useless...all useless garbage."

When all seems hopeless, his cellphone rings. He scans the caller ID but doesn't recognize the number,

"Dr. Paul Carol here...

how can I help you?"

Sophia's voice rings out from the phone,

"Dr. Paul...Sophia Miller here...

how are you doing Doc?"

Paul scratches his head,

"To tell you the truth...

feeling like dog meat right now."

"Dog Meat...What's the matter?

I can ALWAYS count on you to

be that upbeat man in my life...

how can I help?"

Paul takes a seat and scratches his curly hair,

"I sure wish you could...I'm stuck

in this damn computer loop Sophia."

"Hey, c'mon now. You're doing

everything you can...and then some,

I'm sure."

The good doctor slams his fist upon his work station,

"But it's not good enough Sophia...

and I don't allow myself failure...

I'm not good at it."

The ever-mothering Sophia reassures him,

"Derrick's gonna wake-up soon

and help you solve this case...

I'm sure of it Paul."

He sits-up a bit taller, encouraged by Sophia's certainty,

"You're right...he IS gonna to

wake-up soon."

He picks up the file that Ellen had coordinated,

"Hey doll...I'm assuming you called about

Ms. Carpenter coming down to my office

to work on her son's letters."

She cuts him off,

"Change of plans...Ellen and I are headed

up to Connecticut for a week or so.

I've sent a complete work-up of Ellen's

information and we'll chat on the phone

for the personal's...if that's okay?"

Paul scans his computer banks...the "NON-COMPLIANT ENCRYPTION" is

still blinking,

"That works perfect...I need a break

from this shit...maybe it'll set me on

a new direction of thought...hmmm...

sounds good...send the rest of her info."

"I already took the liberty Paul.

I knew you'd be a good boy and

do what Sophia asks. Talk to you soon."

"Yes ma'am...I'm on it."

Paul hangs-up then shakes his head lovingly,

"You just gotta love that Sophia."

Opening Ellen's file, he starts to work on the new brainteaser.

Chapter 57

After seeing Ellen and Sophia safely home, Scott put his D.A.'s hat

on tightly. From meetings all day with the Chief of the N.J. State Police, to

a full press-conference that night with the Governor, he's run the gambit.

It's after midnight at the Crime Lab's Morgue and Scott's talking with the

longtime Medical Examiner, Dr. Anthony Gianotto. The salty veteran and

Scott walk down the cold, sterile corridor,

"Well...let me show you what

I'm talking about Scottie-boy...

got him put back together in

Drawer #6."

They continue their trek, heading towards the bank of drawers housing

corpses, but not before Dr. Anthony stops at a small break-station.

Opening the microwave door, he grabs a warmed bowl of lima bean and

avocado porridge as Scott grimaces,

"How can you eat that stuff Tony?"

Anthony grabs a spoon and wolfs-down a large bite, smiling the whole

time with glee. He wipes his mouth on his sleeve while chuckling,

"You still can't stomach the stiffs,

huh Scott? Well, let's go meet

your buddy."

Upon reaching Drawer #6 Dr. Anthony reaches out, pulls it open then sets his bowl of porridge on the drawer's edge. Sliding back the sheet, Tony reveals a yet to be identified Luc...and the sight of him, after a thirty foot fall, makes Scott wince. Anthony picks right up on the opportunity to make his friend squirm,

"Damn...look, he's fallen all to pieces."

Anthony laughs then takes another big bite of porridge. He points to where the hunk of wood penetrated Luc's chest cavity,

"Makes me remember when I

used to put Tabasco in my porridge."

Poking at Luc's corpse and laughing,

"Same basic consistency too."

Anthony stomps his foot as Scott barks,

"You've been doing this shit

tooooo long Tony...that's some

nasty stuff right there buddy."

Anthony grabs his side trying to contain himself,

"Right on both accounts Scott,

but back to our friend here...

no tattoos, not one remarkable

mole or birthmark."

Anthony points at Luc's face,

"Obviously...he's of Haitian descent."

The doctor picks up a file and looks through its contents,

"From his dental scan I know that

he's had work done in Haiti,

as recently as three years ago.

The dentists do some crazy

bridgework down there...I'm

sure it wasn't done here in the States"

Scott jots down a few notes as Anthony continues,

"My best guesstimate Scott...

without any ID on him and

no ICE papers from Haiti..."

Anthony puts Luc's file aside,

"...you're gonna need a damn

big break to nail this one

down buddy."

Scott raps Anthony on the arm,

"Thanks for coming out this late Tony...

the Governor's Office is wedged so far

up my ass that I can barely breathe."

The old friends share a look of condolence as Anthony slides the lid closed

on Drawer #6, and Luc Detaile', for good.

Chapter 58

Sunday morning is filled with new hope as Ellen and Sophia ready themselves for the trip up to Connecticut. Watching Ellen pack her clothes and chat-away with Scott on the phone, it fills Sophia's heart with the satisfaction of a matchmaking job well done. But this new couple's quick and remarkably deep connection has even taken Sophia by surprise,

"Am I great matchmaker or what?"

Sophia asks herself while tidying up.

Her attentive gaze is noticed by Ellen,

"What?"

Caught off guard, Sophia then whimsically tosses one of Ellen's T-shirts over to her,

"It's nothing honey...just that through

all this madness, you and Scott are just

too cute."

She waves-off Sophia's statement then says to Scott,

"Gotta finish getting ready...

I'll call you when we're on

the road."

Ellen turns to shield Sophia from the "Smoooooooch" that she sends his

way. Hanging up the phone and without any hesitation,

"I know...we are too cute."

Under handing her throw, Ellen lobs the T-shirt back to Sophia and in a

bad "Old English" voice,

"I'm not taking that one me Lady...

do appreciate the sentiment

though my darling."

Sophia bows her head and courtesy's to her friend's gesture,

"You just reminded me of my Stephanie.

Packing for a weekend getaway and

yapping to one of her beaus on the

phone."

"Thank you for that Sophia."

"For what?"

"For making all this death...

all of this god-damned death

and murder...and I'm so, so

frightened...but you make it

all bearable Sophia."

Dashing over to Sophia, Ellen then hugs her dearly,

> "I know that I should be trembling...
>
> but you and Scott always make me
>
> feel safe."

Sophia pulls back, smiles and carefully moves aside a few stray hairs from Ellen's eyes,

> "I know that I should want to close
>
> off from the rest of the world Sophia...
>
> but you've opened up my heart to
>
> this wonderful man...and so many
>
> emotions that haven't stirred inside
>
> me in forever and a day."

Ellen wipes a small tear from Sophia's eye,

> "I love you Sophia Miller."

Sophia begins to cry, but then catches herself and lightly smack Ellen's rear-end,

> "Well I love you too Ms. Carpenter...
>
> so let's get your little butt up to
>
> Connecticut and up to safety, okay?"
>
> "Okay mom...I mean Sophia...

whoops."

A deeply touched Sophia reaches over and places a kiss upon Ellen's forehead,

"Shhhh...Mom it is."

Both smiling, they wipe their eyes then get back to packing.

About an hour later and now on-the-road, Sophia mashes on the accelerator pedal of her Lincoln Town-Car, speeding into the fast-lane of the highway. Ellen gets settled in the passenger seat, adjusts her bandages then asks,

"Taking I-95 to 91?"

Sophia sets the cruise control and eases back into the driver's seat,

"Exactly...that's when I drive why

I love leaving so early on a Sunday.

It should be smooth sailing all the

way up there."

Ellen takes a sip of her coffee as Sophia inquires,

"So...what's on the agenda when

we get there? I know that you are

familiar with most of the area.

It must seem like only yesterday

when you first took Tommy there

to see the campus."

Ellen flashes to a sweet memory and smiles,

"That first day Sophia, when Tommy

saw those ivy-covered walls and that

wonderful look on his face...

it made every struggle to get him

there totally worth it."

Sophia nods her heads in agreement as Ellen continues,

"Plus I'd really like to go to the campus.

Those sweet letters from those two

professors who wrote to me after

Tommy passed...I just have to thank

them in person."

Sophia taps the steering wheel,

"Well then, meet the two

professors we shall."

A thought comes to Sophia's mind,

"Plus, you are simply going to adore

Scott's place. He scooped it up three

years ago and I do believe that it's just

perfect...for this new couple that I know."

"You just don't ever stop...do ya Sophia?"

They share a laugh as the Town-Car motors up I-95.

Chapter 59

While adjusting his car radio, LeSean changes lanes on his way
back home to Staten Island. He stops scanning as a bulletin blares out
from a news station,

"...and the attack by the young Haitian

was thwarted by an employee of the

District Attorney's office and a fast

thinking State Trooper. It has been

speculated that the two attacks

upon Detective Hayes's life were

related to a string of robberies

and murders Statewide spanning

over the last year.

To repeat, a young man fell to

his death while attempting an

assassination at Memorial General..."

LeSean turns down the radio and soaks-in the valuable piece of info,

"Well thank you 1010 Win News...

you probably just saved my

black ass."

He spots a Rest Stop sign in the distance then weaves through traffic to make the highway turnoff,

"I just need some stiff java...

figure out what this crazy

Haitian's got planned for me...

gonna have to beat Philippe

to the punch. Life in the jungle...

kill or be killed."

Pulling into the Rest Stop, LeSean prepares for the upcoming confrontation with his Haitian counterpart. Reaching down between the center console and driver's seat, LeSean wields his oversized carpet knife,

"Nuttin' cuts skin like ol'

faithful here."

He mimics cutting someone's throat,

"Just gotta take care of the

upstairs situation first...then

onto Philippe."

After stuffing the knife back into the crevice, he jumps out of his ride and heads for his coffee.

Chapter 60

Scott's just finishing brushing his teeth and is about to apply some shaving cream when his cellphone rings,

"Never fails…every time

you're getting ready."

He rinses off the handful of cream, eyes Dr. Paul's name on his caller ID and grabs the phone,

"Paul...what's happening Doc?"

"Scott...you got to get down to

the hospital right away.

Derrick's vitals indicate he may

come out of his coma anytime.

I just knew that you'd want to

be here when it happens."

Scott checks the time on his phone,

"You there already?"

"Bedside with my brother...

now get your ass down here."

Scott adjusts his towel and tells him emphatically,

"On my way, just finishing up here...."

and thanks Paulie."

He hangs up, quickly dials Ellen's number and it goes directly to her

voicemail,

"Hey girls, got some encouraging news

about Derrick. I'll call you both later

and let you know...Love ya."

Scott finishes his message, shakes his head then says aloud,

"Love ya...hmmm."

He looks towards the heavens,

"Thank you."

Scott skips the shaving and quickly gets ready to head over to the hospital.

Chapter 61

It's been a long sleepless night, followed by an agonizing morning

for Philippe. Still lying atop Luc's bedroom's futon, he slowly sharpens the

knife intended for LeSean's undoing,

"How did I let LeSean even bring-up

the notion of Luc trying it...I knew

he wasn't ready."

He artfully tosses the knife across Luc's room and it lodges it into a

photograph hanging on the wall, shattering the frame's glass. He begins to

lightly sob with the acceptance of Luc's death...but that sentiment is

quickly broken upon hearing a squeak in the stairwell leading down from

Grannie's,

"Oh shit...it's ON."

With a cat-like deftness he slides from the bed, slithers over then pulls the

knife from the wall...but the crackling of glass under his feet freezes him in

place. Philippe's mind races,

"Has LeSean come home early?

Has he heard about Luc's death

on the news?"

Jumping over the remaining shards of glass, he lands next to the door leading into the living room.

The only light illuminating the darkened apartment is from Grannie's stairwell...and she NEVER leaves that door open. Just as he slides out of the bedroom, the resounding crash of LeSean's fist onto his jaw sends Philippe reeling. That first smash is followed by two rib shattering kicks, but luckily Philippe rolls across his blade and grabs the knife. He flings it into LeSean's abdomen,

"Mother-fucker!" screams LeSean

as he staggers from the impact.

Blood spurts from his open wound as LeSean then tears the knife from his side.

Diving towards the wounded Philippe, they struggle on the floor for supremacy. A gust of wind then closes Grannie's door and completely obscures any view. The utter darkness is filled with the nauseating echoes of someone repeatedly jabbing a knife into flesh.

Finally, the carnage comes to an end as the warmness of freshly spilled blood covers both men. To this victor comes the ultimate of spoils because in the complete blackness of that basement apartment, only one continues inhaling the sweet breath of life.

Chapter 62

Dr. Paul's discussing the patient chart with the Attending Physician as Scott enters Derrick's room. Scott waves to him then walks over and takes a seat next to Derrick. Paul finishes his conversation with the doctor, taps him on the shoulder then the young Resident leaves the room. Taking a seat next to Derrick,

"So...what's the deal Paulie?"

Paul takes a seat on the opposite side of the bed,

"It's all looking good...he's just

gotta wake-up, plain and simple."

Scott shakes his head an understanding yes as he strokes Derrick's arm,

"C'mon buddy...you can do this."

Paul readjusts the blankets just as Derrick's eyes begin to flutter. Paul notices the event and enthusiastically roots Derrick on,

"I know you have it in ya brother...

c'mon, I love you man...you can do it!"

Derrick creases his eyes open and in a soft voice responds,

"Just as always...my man Paul's

a big fuckin' mush."

Scott and Paul emphatically stand, high-five each other across Derrick's

bed as Scott yells out,

> "Get someone in here...he's awake!"

They both turn their attention to Derrick as he reaches up then grabs

Paul's forearm,

> "Gotta...tell you...what...I remember."

Paul says to Derrick,

> "They'll be time for all that buddy."

Derrick clenches tighter upon Paul's arm,

> "No..."

Derrick looks over at Scott and in a rasped voice,

> "Hey there...Scott...
>
> you both have to know..."

A medical team barges into the room and attempts to maneuver around

Scott and Paul. Derrick defiantly barks with all of his available strength,

> "Wait..."

The team halts their procedures as Derrick pulls his friends closer,

> "Luc...and Philippe Detaile'...
>
> get em'."

Derrick slowly raises his fist...he's met with Scott and Paul both giving him

a fist-pump in return. They quickly slip out of the Medical Team's way and

while walking over to the door Scott relays,

"Detaile'...that's Haitian...

gotta be the link Paul."

Paul nods in agreement,

"Go do your thing Scott...I've got it all

handled here. I'll text you with every

update of our boy's condition."

The Medical Team attends to Derrick as Paul pumps his fist in the air and

yells,

"Way to go brother-man!"

Chapter 63

Hanging-up a few of Ellen's dresses in the master bedroom closet of Scott's Connecticut home, Sophia calls out to her lying upon the bed,

"So, Derrick's out of his coma...

that's terrific" Sophia cheers.

Walking out of the closet, she heads over to a pile of clothes on the end of the king-sized bed just as Ellen rolls over,

"Yup, Scott just texted that Dr. Paul

is going to stay at the hospital, but

he's sprinting back to the D.A's office...

seems that Derrick remembered

something vital about the case."

Sophia begins to store undergarments into a dresser as Ellen continues,

"Scott's got a meeting this afternoon

with the detective who's taken over

the investigation...they've got a great

lead on identifying the Haitian guy

who kicked me in the chest."

"Wow...that's fantastic."

Taking a seat on the bed next to Ellen,

"So...tell me honey...how

are you feeling?"

Ellen shrugs her shoulders,

"Now that we're all settled-in...

I am feeling better. I'm tired,

but definitely glad to be

outta Jersey."

Beaming with motherly care, Sophia strokes Ellen's hair,

"How about you take a quick cat-nap?

I'll finish setting-up here...then we'll

head into town for a late lunch?"

Ellen thinks for a moment,

"A nap would be dynamite...

and afterwards we can grab a bite..."

With a childlike delight, Ellen snuggles the blankets,

"...and if we feel up to it, we'll head

over to the college...okay?"

She playfully grabs Ellen's foot,

"Whatever you want honey."

Ellen delicately turns on her side as Sophia pulls the blanket to cover her. Ellen mumbles,

"Just a quick catnap...okay?

Then we'll head out to the city."

"Anything you want sweetie."

Chapter 64

Leaning back into his office chair, Scott discusses the merits of the case with the young detective that's been assigned to handle the case,

"I also wanted to tell you sir,

how honored I am that you chose

me for this assignment."

Scott surveys his "Service Record" file,

"Timothy J. Bowdish---Detective

of Major Crimes"

Scrolling through Bowdish's file, he's impressed by all the commendations packing Tim's dossier.

"And thank you sir for the access

to all of Derrick's files. That computer

setup he has in his Mercedes...

it's awesome to say the least."

"No problem Detective...and by

the way, it's Scott.

Reading your file...seems like you've

followed Derrick's playbook...almost

down to the letter."

Again scanning Bowdish's file,

> "From a troubled past, to first in
>
> your class...
>
> making Lead Detective of Vice
>
> in two years."

Tim's taken aback by Scott's respect,

> "Thank you sir...I mean Scott.
>
> We've got everybody and
>
> their mother looking for Detaile'...
>
> it's only a matter of time."

Scott taps his lips with his forefinger,

> "Anything else?"

Just as Scott asks, his phone rings.

> "Scott Phillips here."

From the other side of the phone,

> "D.A. Phillips...this is Sergeant
>
> Weems of the New York State
>
> Police. My Chief requested that
>
> I call you when we got any news
>
> on the Detaile' situation."

"One second officer…

I'm putting you on speaker."

Activating the button,

"What do you have for me Sergeant?"

There's a slight pause in the Sergeant's answer as he tries to choke-out a

response,

"I'm at the Detaile's residence. The judge

finally okayed the search warrant…

in all my years…I never…

it's a bloodbath sir."

Scott calculates for a moment,

"Thank the Chief for the head's-up

Sergeant, we'll be over soon."

After clicking off the phone he turns back to Bowdish,

"This is your first Major Crimes

homicide case, correct Detective?"

With confidence, Bowdish stiffens his posture,

"True…but I did work Vice for the last

five…and by the way Scott, its Tim."

Impressed with the young detective' brimming confidence, Scott makes

mental notes as Tim continues,

> "Derrick's one of the main reasons I
>
> became a cop. I saw an article about
>
> him, years ago in the Star Ledger.
>
> Being an orphan too, his story inspired
>
> me to make something of myself...
>
> and get the hell off those
>
> mean streets Derrick talked about."

Scott stands and leads the way,

> "Well, let's get this first one under
>
> your belt Detective...I mean Tim."

They share a handshake then head to the Detaile's.

Chapter 65

Seated at a booth on a Yale campus Starbuck's, Ellen and Sophia share a large slice of chocolate cheesecake. Ellen's nap has done her a world of good, and they idly chat about the surroundings.

A young man passes them, stops in his tracks and does a double-take at Ellen. Thinking for a moment on where he's met this beautiful lady before, it then comes to his mind,

"Excuse me ma'am...Your Mrs. Carpenter…

Tommy's mom, right?"

Ellen's attention is drawn from her ongoing conversation,

"Yes...I'm Tommy's mom...

and you are?"

The young student completes his way over to their table,

"I'm sorry...I'm Winston Dillard.

Tommy and I had adjacent room's

our freshman and sophomore years."

"Oh, I remember you Winston...

looks like you've grown six inches."

Ellen notices her social faux-pas and introduces her friend,

"Winston, this is my dear friend Sophia Miller.

Did you have a question honey?"

"Actually yes Mrs. Carpenter, I did.

I run the campus lost and found.

Over the Christmas break, they

cleared Tommy's room and stored

his personals at my office.

Could you make it over and claim

his items? It's right at the end of

the street here."

Flashing him an "okay" sign,

"Of course...we'll be there in an

hour or so, okay?"

"That would be great.

And I'm so sorry for your loss

Tommy was such a great guy.

Just so you know, they held a vigil

of remembrance in the main quad

for Tommy after Winter break."

Now beaming to the revelation of Winston's sweet news,

"I didn't know that Winston...how wonderful.

Thank you dear and we'll see you soon."

Winston waves his goodbyes and scampers off as Ellen looks to Sophia for

guidance,

"That's okay with you Sophia, right?"

Waving her question off,

"Of course it is. We'll just grab the bull

by the horns, bring Tommy's stuff back

to Scott's and sort it all out there."

Sophia grabs her fork and takes a sizable hunk of the cheesecake sitting

between them,

"But let's finish this yummy cake

first, shall we? Then we'll get down

to business."

Ellen takes a swig of her coffee then joins Sophia in their dessert.

Chapter 66

Dabbing a small amount of Vapor-Rub under his nose, Scott offers the same to Tim as they enter Grannie Detaile's top-floor apartment. Tim thanks him, but then waves-off his gesture as Scott is still affected by the strong odor,

"I will never get used to it Detective...

that smell of death."

From behind him and catching wind of Scott's admission, Dr. Gianotto laughs aloud,

"Weak Stomach Phillips...

that's his name..."

Instantly recognizing Dr. Tony's smart-ass repertoire, Scott finishes the quote,

"One foul whiff...

and puking's my game."

Looking over his shoulder,

"How's the hammer hangin' Tony?"

The coroner comes around Scott and they shake hands,

"So...who's your sidekick here Scott?

Looks a little green to me."

Scott pats Tim on the shoulder,

      "Dr. Anthony Gianotto, meet Detective

      Timothy J. Bowdish.

      Tim, this is Dr. Tony…my goomba

      and all around good egg. Our

      crime spree has crossed state lines

      so I've asked the Feds bring in Dr. Tony."

Tony reaches out and shakes Tim's hand,

      "I see you're not wearing any of

      Scott's under-nose-potion…

      a man after my own heart.

      Bet you love a good gory

      crime scene…yes?"

Tim quickly quips,

      "Do fat babies fart Doc?"

Tony looks over at Scott,

      "Oh, Scottie my boy…

      I really like this kid."

Waving in the direction of Grannie's Lazy-Boy,

      "Well this crime scene my young friend…

it just might take your breath away.

C'mon boys, let me show you what

I'm talking about."

The three walk across the apartment and over to Granny's favorite chair

that's covered with a blood-stained sheet. Tony abruptly rips off the

soaked-linen revealing Grannie's gaping neck wound. A completely

captivated Tim's eyes widen,

"Wow, that's intense. Some serious

anger issues with this one Doc, huh?"

Quickly retorting,

"Really kid...and here I thought it was

a fucking suicide."

Tony slaps the green-pea on the shoulder as a nearly decapitated Grannie

causes Scott to turn green.

Engrossed by the morbid spectacle, Dr. Tony and Tim lean in closer to

inspect Granny's dramatic gashes,

"That's some serious shit right there Dr. G...

the force involved in a single-strike like this

is incredible. I'm gonna say a very large

carpet knife."

Tony agrees and points his finger near Grannie's chin,

> "Very good...you've noticed there's a smooth
>
> line to the incision. No doubt about it Detective,
>
> her assailant must have slid up from behind
>
> and in one dramatic slash, cut this poor lady's
>
> head nearly clean-off."

Backing away from the body, they both turn to Scott,

> "And just wait boys, we're just getting started.
>
> You're gonna love the handiwork that's waiting
>
> for you in the basement apartment."

Tim claps his hands,

> "Can't wait Dr. G...let's get at it."

Tony slaps Scott on the back,

> "Like I said...this kid's gonna fit right in.
>
> Derrick would love this guy."

Traveling the ten feet to the stairwell, they all descend into this morning's death-match. As they reach the bottom of the stairs, Tony informs them,

> "Just stay behind the taped lines down
>
> here fellas...they're still testing all the
>
> various blood pools."

Scott sees the mutilated corpse sprawled upon the blood soaked floor,

"Ah shit, don't tell me."

Tony informs Scott,

"That's stiff number two, Philippe Detaile'.

Thirty-three major punctures marks and a

countless number of defensive wounds.

This one was personal Scottie boy.

Look at the ferocity in the strike at the

entry points?"

Tim crouches to get a better vantage point as a discouraged Scott says,

"Holy shit Tony...I can't catch a break.

Philippe here was the only direct lead

to my mystery man number three.

Maybe we'll get lucky with some prints

or blood."

Rising to his feet, Tim asks,

"Scott, now that interrogating Philippe

is definitely outta the question, do you

think it would be bad-form for me to

stop by the hospital? I'd like to see

how Detective Hayes is doing...

maybe pick his brain a little...

if he's up to it."

The D.A. shakes his head in agreement,

"Excellent idea Detective, like you

said...only if he's up to it though.

I know Derrick would love to get

back into the game and contribute."

"Great...thanks Scott."

Scott's seen enough of this slaughterhouse and prepares to head back to

his office,

"I'm outta here...I'll just leave you

two weird ghouls to go and have

your fun."

Scott heads back to the stairwell as Tim and Tony continue discussing the

many details of the crime scene.

Chapter 67

LeSean's changing the gauze on his self-sutured stab wound as he sits upon his apartment's sofa, watching television. He takes-in a deep drag of a joint, then slowly exhales,

"You are one smart mother-fucker

LeSean."

After another toke,

"Every loose end has been tied-up

and you've got all the cash.

Just lay low for a few months...

jump back to the safety deposit

box then permanently disappear

into the night."

There's a loud banging at his apartment's door and a familiar voice barks out,

"LeSean...I know you're in there!"

The pounding on the door continues,

"It's your old buddy...Parole Officer

Nelson...here with the Staten

Island Police...open up asshole!"

The thumping gets louder as LeSean quickly assesses the situation and determines there's nowhere for him to run,

> "I'm comin'...hold your mutha-fuckin'
>
> horses already!"

He swallows the blunt, meanders over to the door and swings it open. Flanked by two very large Police Officers, the confidently striding P. O. Nelson enters his apartment. Taking in an animated breath through his nose,

> "Tsk, tsk, tsk...smells like somebody's
>
> been having a little party in here."

Waving-off Nelson's notion,

> "Well what ya know...it's my
>
> fuckin' P.O."

LeSean flops himself back upon his couch in defiance,

> "What's it this time Nelson? I'm
>
> clean as a whistle and in less than
>
> a month...I'll never have to see
>
> your monkey-ass again."

Nelson snaps his fingers and coyly responds,

> "Ah, one month...funny you should

mention that Mr. Jeffries. Because,

that's how long the Department of

Corrections is going to be housing

you my friend."

He indicates for the officers to place LeSean in handcuffs. The two

military-cut behemoths comply and yank LeSean from the couch,

"What the fuck...this is bullshit Nelson

and you know it."

The larger of the two officers completes the task of slamming LeSean to

the floor and cuffing him.

"Bullshit or not, what this IS

about is your fucking stupidity

Jeffries...you violated your parole

ass-wipe."

After being jerked to his feet, Nelson slaps him across the face and directs

them to take him away,

"You shouldn't have gone down to

Baltimore LeSean...now get this dumb

ass piece of shit outta my sight boys."

Again they follow orders and drag him to the front door. LeSean matter-of-factly barks,

> "I'll do this one-month-short standing
>
> on my damn head...
>
> you fuckin' douchebag."

As the officers drag LeSean away, Nelson notices something with an elastic band wedged in corner of the sofa,

> "My my...what do we
>
> have here?"

He reaches down and pulls out a large wad of hundred dollar bills,

> "Bingo."

The two officers wait patiently outside the front door as Nelson jams the wad into his pants pocket. LeSean screams from the outside of his apartment,

> "What the fuck you looking for
>
> Nelson...c'mon and take me
>
> to the hole."

Nelson laughs and says to himself,

> "I'll just take this for safe-keeping...
>
> I'm sure he won't miss it."

Nelson bounces over to the front door,

"Let's hit it guys...like he said...

lets get his ass to the hole."

Chapter 68

Later that same Sunday evening and now back at the Connecticut house, the girls are just finishing sifting through Tommy's returned items. Sophia completes folding a deep-blue, Yale hoodie then places it into a large box they've marked "Tommy's Clothes". Ellen notices her actions,

"Could you leave that one out Sophia?

That's the first thing I bought for Tommy

at the bookstore his freshman year."

Sophia pulls the sweatshirt out of the box,

"Of course, whatever you want."

Ellen walks over, takes the hoodie and slides it over her head. Taking in a deep breath, she drifts-off into a sweet memory...

...Tommy can barely be seen over the pile of books he's carrying as Ellen waits patiently at the cash register of the bookstore. He carefully sets everything down on the checkout counter. Spotting that blue hoodie hanging next to the front door, she runs over and snatches it off the display,

"Mom...you've spent enough already...

you don't..."

Ellen puts her finger to his mouth, stopping him in mid-sentence,

"Shssssh...This is what Mom's do

Thomas...so zip it mister."

After placing the sweatshirt next to the other items, she puts her arm

around him,

"Just let me enjoy...okay?"

Thomas recants his objections as the attendant rings up the items. Ellen

drifts back to reality...

..."Ellen...Ellen honey...where'd you go?" asks Sophia.

"Just remembering that sweet kid of mine."

Ellen slides her hands into the hoodie's front pocket, feels a piece of

paper and pulls out a small note,

"Chelsea and Spud...

10:30am 01/15 appt.

Dr. Turner"

Ellen hands the note to Sophia as she takes a seat on the bed,

"Definitely Tommy's handwriting.

What could it mean?"

Ellen thinks for a moment then remembers the picture of Tommy and

Chelsea with their dog Spud. Grabbing her purse from the top of the

mahogany bureau, she reaches into it and pulls out her keychain,

"Look, Chelsea and her dog Spud...

they must have had a Veterinarian

appointment set for January fifteenth."

Sophia longs for more info on Tommy's mystery girl,

"Ooooo...I wonder who this Chelsea

really is?"

"Yeah...like does she go to Yale?

Were her and Tommy really serious?

I'd have a million questions for her."

Sophia lies back on the bed and places her hands behind her head,

"I've got it."

She quickly sits up and snaps her fingers,

"We'll ask Dr. Paul to help us track

her down. Maybe finding Chelsea

will help us figure out what Tommy's

been trying to tell you."

"But I haven't finished putting together

Tommy's information for the meeting

with him yet."

Sophia cuts Ellen off,

"I took the "liberty" of finishing your file

for Dr. Paul and already sent it over to

his office...hope you don't mind?"

"Mind? Hey silly...you're the best

friend a girl could have...always

thinking of what's best for me."

Sophia takes a snapshot of the note with her phone then emails it over to

Dr. Paul,

"I'm sending the note over to him

right now...Detective Sophia Miller's

on the case."

Chapter 69

Seated across the desk from Dr. Gayle Andrews, Alexis finishes signing the last in a group of official looking documents. After completing her final John Hancock's, she hands the clipboard over to the doctor. Flipping through, then double-checking Alexis' paperwork,

"Perfect" she says setting

the clipboard aside.

Feigning a sweet endearing smile, Alexis revels in the fact that Dr. Andrews has unwittingly followed her plan to the letter. The doctor shows genuine concern,

"Alexis, I'd be remiss if I didn't inform you...

of the recent troubles at one of our prisons."

With false-empathy, Alexis nods her head slowly,

"That's exactly it Dr. Andrews...

that's why I've endowed the money

from the charity fund. My parents

being Holocaust survivors, would have

wanted to make a tangible difference...

where it's sorely needed."

Dr. Andrews is completely in the dark, having nary a clue into Alexis'

ulterior motives. The large monetary donation that she's endowed has

given Alexis carte blanche...so she can do relief work at the penitentiary of

her choice. Alexis leans in closer to the doctor,

"And that's why I've chosen to serve food

to these poor, hapless young men. They've

mostly been dealt, from the start, a bum-hand

and if I can make even a modicum of change...

I've made a huge difference."

"That was just beautiful Ms. Weinstein,

and after what you've been through...

I thought I was the only one who really

cared about the welfare of these inmates."

Catching herself pouring out emotion,

"Listen to me blubbering. I apologize for...."

Alexis waves off the doctor's apology,

"No sorry's needed Doctor..."

Checking her watch,

"...but if we are done here, I really

do have a pressing appointment

that I can't miss."

"Oh...of course. Again, our deepest

thanks and condolences to you

Ms. Weinstein."

After shaking hands, Alexis turns and flashes a "cat that ate the canary".

Chapter 70

Ellen wakes abnormally late on this beautiful Monday morning, then takes notice of the 9:43 a.m. on her alarm clock. After a full stretch and yawn, she rolls over and is face-to-face with a still slumbering Sophia,

"Well, good morning to you

Miss Sunshine" she whispers.

Creeping out of the large bed, Ellen slips into her old slippers and sets off to make the morning's coffee. Reaching the kitchen, she goes to grab the bag of Dunkin' Donuts coffee off the counter but then freezes in place, hearing a groaning noise in the next room,

"What the hell was that?"

Cautiously making her way across the kitchen, she peers around the passageway leading to the neighboring room...then smiles after spotting Scott soundly asleep on the living room sofa.

Tip-toeing over to him, she clears a group of papers from near his feet then kisses him lightly on the cheek. Slipping niftily back to the kitchen, Ellen waves at Sophia who has already started making the morning's coffee,

"That man of ours is so sweet" Ellen brags.

He must have slipped in here late last night,

saw us sleeping and crashed on the couch.

Looked like from the file he was working on

it must have been a long night."

Scott lumbers into the kitchen, rubs his eyes and smells the brewing

ambrosia,

"Were you two chickadees just talkin' bout

me? Swear my ears were burning."

Like a bear waking from an extended hibernation, he yawns while

stretching out his large frame,

"Mmm...that smells wonderful."

He steps over to Ellen, takes her in his arms then dramatically dips her,

just like during their dance at Mario's. While he's still dangling her, with

his free hand Scott pulls a pack of Wintergreen Tic-Tac's from his pocket

and rattles the plastic container. He pops one in his mouth,

"Tic-Tac's are just MADE

for early-morning-necking."

Slowly raising Ellen back to her feet, they share a beautiful kiss.

"So...what's on the schedule girls?

I've got the whole day off."

Ellen and Scott instinctively look over to their mother hen for the answer.

Sophia, seemingly in cahoots with Scott, winks at him,

> "Well, I've got a beautiful day planned for
>
> you two...you're going to love it.
>
> And as for me..."

Smiling coyly,

> "...I've got some sleuthing to handle
>
> with Tommy's new clue. I've got a
>
> hunch that I'm gonna follow-up on."

Scott is surprised to hear about the new info,

> "You girls found something useful in all
>
> Thomas' stuff? That's great."

Brimming with excitement, Ellen shows him the note of Tommy's,

> "Yeah baby, like finding a needle
>
> in the haystack. I found this note
>
> about Chelsea in one of Tommy's
>
> sweatshirts."

Sophia chimes in,

> "Dr. Paul and I have a plan in the
>
> works to track down her dog Spud,

through a database of local

veterinarians...and hopefully,

we'll find Chelsea in the process."

Scott snaps his fingers,

"Well then...seems like you two have

it all handled."

Scott pours the ladies, then himself, their cups of coffee. Raising their

mugs, they clink them together and toast to the wonderful day.

Chapter 71

That long penitentiary-walk, where the newly incarcerated are paraded in a line before the incumbent inmates, is no stranger to LeSean Jeffries. While being harassed and heckled, he confidently strides towards his cell with the sense that he owns the place.

Just as he enters his new accommodations, Frankie Botelli reaches from inside one of the neighboring cages and grabs LeSean's sleeve,

"Good to see you back Jeffries...

Renee wants to see you...ASAP!

He heard what happened to his

two cousins...hell to pay old friend."

LeSean rips away Frankie's grip,

"You tell Renee I had nothing to do

with that shit...that's what I'm doing

back here...I was shacked up in

Baltimore with my baby momma

at the time."

Reaching his hands through the bars, LeSean shoves Frankie across his cell,

"Tell him to ask the cops if he doesn't

fuckin' believe me."

Frankie stumbles backwards, catches himself then shoots LeSean the middle finger,

"Fuck You LeSean...I aint your errand boy...

not my fuckin' neck on the line."

After his brief scuffle, LeSean and the other new inmates are directed to their new accommodations. With his confidence now shaken, LeSean paces back and forth across his new cell. Echoing into his room, he can faintly hear Botelli's high-pitched voice,

"Jeffries...Renee's comin' for you."

Dropping to his cot, LeSean places his head in his hands,

"How could I fuckin' forget that?"

He's missed taking into account the one critical detail holding him back from escaping for good...Renee Batiste.

Chapter 72

Sophia's car horn beeps as she drives down the Connecticut house's winding driveway, then turns left onto the main drag. Ellen and Scott finish waving their goodbye's to Sophia and he tenderly grabs her hand.

Gazing up at him, they kiss on the walkway leading back to the house...just as a passing rain shower decides to unleash a near torrent. Unfazed by the downpour, they're protected by a seemingly impenetrable shield and all of the world's madness.

With drops of rainwater hanging from the tip of his nose, Scott cups her dampened face in his hands,

"Sugar...let's jump inside and get

outta the rain...you're shivering."

Ellen pulls Scott closer, hugs him and whispers,

"Shivering...definitely."

She pulls back and stares into his eyes,

"But, there's no place that I'd rather be...

than here in your arms."

Another quick kiss Ellen waves,

"C'mon baby, let's go dry off."

They link hands and scamper, like school kids, up the walkway and into the house.

Toweling-off from her shower, Ellen checks her appearance in the master bathroom's mirror. Scott taps on the door,

"You decent in there sugar?"

Ellen smiles at her reflection,

"Of course silly bear...

this IS your house."

He walks through the bathroom's doorway and is amazed to see how the rain has changed Ellen's hair from straight to curly. Scott thinks,

"Am I lucky or what to have this

beauty...in just a bath-towel

and alone in my bathroom."

Walking around, then up from behind him, she gently caresses his muscular arms,

"Did you need something Mr.

District Attorney?"

Scott abruptly turns then draws her near,

"When I saw you and Sophia safely

asleep in my bed...it was the first

time I felt in control since this

whole craziness began."

She strokes Scott's cheek as he continues,

"When I first got the news of what

happened in Derrick's room...and

I wasn't there to protect you...I

vowed that if you'd let me Ellen,

I'd never let anyone ever hurt

you again."

Looking into her eyes,

"I realize that we've known each

other casually for years, but these

last few weeks...they've changed

my life in a way I never expected.

I Love You Ellen Carpenter and I

want you in my life forever.

Please, leave New Jersey for

good and let's try to make this

OUR home."

Left speechless, the thoughts of sharing a life with this wonderful man, has taken her breath away. Scott stammers in response to her silence,

"Ah shit…too much too soon?"

Finally regaining the power of speech, Ellen throws her arms around Scott,

"I love you too sweetie! You've

made me so incredibly happy."

Ellen wipes her tears away,

"I'd love to give this a go…

so YES, is definitely my

final answer."

Like a child receiving that perfect Christmas gift, Scott sweeps-up then carries Ellen through the doorway and places her upon the bed. As Ellen slowly removes her towel, Scott's nearly overwhelmed by his desire. She then seductively bites her bottom lip and urges him closer with her pointer finger,

"I want you…inside of me."

After gently sliding atop, then inside of her, he looks into her sparkling green eyes,

"There's no place in the world that I'd rather be."

Chapter 73

Sophia pulls her Town-Car into an available parking-spot at Dr. Turner's Veterinarian Office. It happens to be the fourth, and last Dr. Turner available on her clues-list. With exasperation, she tells Dr. Paul over her speakerphone,

"Dr. Paul, I just pulled into

the parking lot...I hope we

have better luck here."

Rolling her eyes,

"It's the last Dr. Turner on our list."

Paul attempts to prop-up Sophia's shaken enthusiasm,

"Don't worry Sophia, this isn't an

exact science. We're going with

our best hypothesis and we'll

follow this lead source until it

bear's fruit, or not. Plus, I'm

working on that photo you sent

me of Chelsea...that should help

me to track her down."

Sophia answers,

"Okay doc."

"Now go in there like you own

the joint Sophia...and don't be

afraid to let them know this does

pertain to an ongoing murder

investigation and you are there

as a rep from my office."

Sophia looks at herself in the rear-view mirror,

"Thanks Paul, for all the support...

you're the best."

Paul whimsically states,

"I KNOW...but seriously, I have a

meeting here for the next few hours,

so please call me tonight. I want to

get your input on my take of Tommy's

clues. I'll have my analysis ready for

you then."

Sophia opens her car door,

"Sounds great, I'll call you."

Sophia hangs-up the phone, swings her door shut and heads towards Dr. Turner's front door. After patiently waiting for a few minutes in the reception room,

"Ms. Miller, how do you do?

I'm Dr. James Turner...my

assistant tells me you're here

on some official business from

New Jersey?"

Sophia walks over and firmly shakes the young doctor's hand. She tells him in a commanding voice while flashing her ID's,

"That's correct...I'm Sophia Miller,

Executive Assistant to District

Attorney Scott Phillips. I'm here

as a representative for Dr. Paul Carol."

The young Vet is impressed with Sophia's credentials,

"What can I do to assist the great

State of New Jersey today?"

"We're looking for assistance in locating this woman."

Ellen shows Dr. Turner a photo of Chelsea, Tommy and Spud,

"If you could just cross-reference your

database for a girl named Chelsea

and a dog named Spud...I believe

he's a Jack Russell Terrier."

The vet complies, begins to type on his keyboard then after a minute of cross-checking,

"I'm sorry Ms. Miller...I don't have

a patient called Spud nor an

owner named Chelsea anywhere

on record."

"Could you try Thomas Carpenter please?'

"Certainly."

He enters Tommy's info,

"Don't have a Thomas Carpenter either

Ms. Miller."

A dejected Sophia shakes Dr. Turner's hand goodbye,

"The State of New Jersey thanks

you for all the cooperation Dr. Turner."

She turns and drags her feet across the office floor...yet another dead

end.

Chapter 74

Still bandaged from the waist down, but sitting upright in his

hospital bed, Derrick waves Detective Bowdish over to him,

"It's Tim Bowdish, right?"

Derrick asks while extending

his hand for a shake.

While clasping hands together Tim responds,

"Nail on the head Detective."

Derrick gestures for Tim to take a seat,

"It's Derrick to you...Scott called

and gave me your info. Glad to

see that you've helped pick-up

the mess I left."

"Mess...are you kidding me?

You've been light-years ahead

of anyone else working on this case.

The Chief's had most of the Division

working on it, and we get nowhere...

you wake-up and we've got two of

three prime suspects spread-out

comfortably in the morgue."

Derrick nods his head and accepts the accolade,

> "Plus that Computer set-up in your
>
> Mercedes...some high-tech shit
>
> Right there Detective."

Winking at Tim,

> "Definitely...my man Dr. Paul set
>
> me up there."

Tim surveys Derrick's bandages,

> "So what's the prognosis on getting
>
> out and hitting the street again?"

Reaching down to strokes his legs,

> "Really, not bad...Doc says six to eight
>
> months of intense rehab and I'll be
>
> up and at 'em."

Tim taps the bed's railing,

> "That's great. I was hoping, maybe
>
> down the road, if you're ever looking
>
> for a partner...Scott and the Chief
>
> said we'd be a great match."

Derrick scratches his chin,

"Definitely something to chew on...

but for now, I'll need you to hit-up

my Computer and enter all known

associates of the Detaile' brothers

starting with the letters LeSe."

Tim enters some info on his smartphone as Derrick continues,

"It may be a first, last or nickname."

Tim completes his note-taking.

"So kid...I heard that the Detaile's

place was a house of horrors."

Tim shakes his head,

"I thought that I saw some shit

during my tour over in Afghanistan...

but this mother fucker is crazy...

he basically cut this grandma's

head off with one swipe."

Derrick nods his head in agreement,

"I also wanted to thank you for

all the access Derrick...most guys

won't let you get near their stuff."

"No thanks necessary kid...just go

get 'em for me. I want you to contact

my associate Dr. Paul Carol over at

Forensics if you need any assistance.

Then call me when you can with

an update...okay?"

Tim stands and salutes Derrick,

"You got it Derrick."

He leaves the room as Derrick then reaches over and fumbles inside his

bedside nightstand drawer. Locating his lucky "METS" hat, Derrick tugs it

onto his head then eases back to watch the ballgame.

Chapter 75

Smiling as she ladles another portion of tonight's dinner onto an inmate's tray, Alexis patiently waits for the right moment for her dress rehearsal. For the test-run, she's chosen a prison over in Staten Island.

Sliding the vial that's hidden up her sleeve into place, Alexis readies to squeeze its contents into her serving ladle...but standing directly in front of her and waiting for his grub is LeSean Jeffries.

As they make direct eye contact, a bone-chilling sensation stands every hair on her body on end. Paralyzed with fear, she stands motionless,

"Can I have my fuckin' slop Missy...

sometime today?"

Somehow, Alexis summons the courage to serve LeSean his portion of beef stew.

As he walks away towards the seating area, LeSean turns and does a double-take of Alexis...he knows that he's seen her before today,

"I never forget a face...

where's do I know that

bitch from?"

Shaking his head, he blows-off the notion then heads to a table.

Unbeknownst to LeSean, he was correct about seeing Alexis before...while ransacking her parent's house, he had mindlessly walked past Alexis' photos a thousand times.

"Did he scare you honey?" asks a
concerned co-worker to a visibly
shaken Alexis. "Go take five and
give yourself a breather...okay?"

"Okay...that sounds good...thanks."

After escaping to a nearby pantry, Alexis grabs each side of her pounding head,

"That's him...I feel it in my bones."

While scarfing down his last piece of bread, LeSean feel's a tap on his left shoulder. He turns to see who it is as Renee artfully slips right behind him,

"I did my checking mother-fucker...
you were in Baltimore when Philippe
got iced. But if I catch a whiff of you
having ANYTHING to do with my family...
you're a dead man LeSean."

LeSean gulps,

"C'mon man...you know I loved

those boys like brothers. After

you helped me get outta here early...

and set up us together...

I mean c'mon Renee...that just

don't make sense."

Renee taps him on the shoulder and mimics cutting LeSean's throat,

"Not even one whiff Jeffries."

With great ferociously, Renee punches LeSean in the ribs,

"Good to see ya old buddy."

As LeSean tries to catch his breath, Renee strides back to a nearby table.

Chapter 76

Scott pours the girls their customary after-dinner Amaretto's on the rocks then sets them on a silver serving tray...right next to a rocks-glass containing three-fingers of his Macallan single-malt scotch. He carries the tray over, sets it on the coffee table and they each grab their respective vessels. Sophia takes the first sip,

> "I'm calling Dr. Paul guys...he had
>
> some things he needed to clarify
>
> about Tommy's note and letters."

A disappointed Sophia apologizes,

> "I'm so sorry Ellen...I really thought
>
> we'd get something useful out of at
>
> least one of those Dr. Turners."
>
> "Oh, sweetie...don't give it another
>
> thought...you really tried."

Quickly interjecting, Scott tries to uplift Sophia,

> "That's the way it works with investigating...
>
> If you hit a brick wall...you bounce off a go in
>
> a different direction. Just remember it's
>
> persistence that beats resistance every time."

Scott winks at Ellen,

>"Plus, you're working with Paul,

>and he's the best. He's humping it

>day and night finding our third assailant."

Sophia turned on her speaker phone so Paul could hear Scott's comments.

Calling-out from over the speaker,

>"Damn straight Scott...it's a wide net we

>cast, but I'm slowly drawing it closed.

>I also wanted to say hello to you Ellen...

>and give you my conclusions about

>Thomas's letters."

She takes a deep breath and readies herself,

>"Sure Dr. Paul...I'm all ears."

>"The way I see it...Tommy was

>getting ready to ask Chelsea to

>marry him. It just fits the pattern...

>graduation, a May wedding.

>And from what Sophia has told me,

>you and Tommy were super close...

>right?"

"Definitely Paul."

"It just makes sense…

a close-to-his-mother kinda guy would

want to make sure that he'd have found

the perfect girl before he sprung her on you…

it's what I probably would have done."

Sophia asks,

"Then why wouldn't she have called Ellen…

when she found out what happened

to Tommy?"

Paul quickly asks,

"Exactly Detective Sophia…why indeed?"

Tapping his fingers on his rocks glass, Scott remarks,

"You're figuring something tragic,

right Paulie?"

Paul answers,

"Give that man a cigar! I'm figuring

some weird coincidence hasn't allowed

her to contact you. We're looking at all

accident and death reports during that

time-frame involving young women

named Chelsea. No nibbles yet, but I'm

thinking of broadening the search,

so I'll keep you up to date.

Have to run, Dr. Paul out."

They sit quietly for a moment, digesting Paul's revelations. Scott breaks

the silence,

"Definitely a chill in the air tonight, huh?

I'm going to start a nice-fire."

Ellen smiles at him,

"That'd be great babe, need any help?"

Scott gently waves her assistance off. He walks over to the fireplace as the

girls settle in for a comfortable evening.

Chapter 77

Tuesday through Thursday's events follow their circadian cycles as our players acquire an odd type of normalcy.

-----Alexis takes a few steps back from serving at the prison. Meeting that inmate and the visceral response that her body and mind had endured…some recalculating is definitely needed if she's going to pull it all off. She's decided to wait until after her group-session on Friday before she goes forward with anything.

-----Ellen browses through store after store, looking for that perfect style for her new three bedroom abode. Antiquing and pattern-swatches transports her to a zone where she hasn't been since Tommy's death…actually happy and content.

-----Tim and Dr. Paul furiously burn the nighttime oil. Hot on the trail of their elusive third assailant, they've narrowed it down to three possibilities…Friday at the prison with LeSean is next on Detective Bowdish's agenda.

-----LeSean has eased right back into prison's three hot's and a cot routine. Comfortable with the fact that he has pulled the wool over the world's eyes, and thankfully Renee's, he readies to finish his month-long stay with the penal system, then finally disappear for good.

-----Scott is adjusting nicely to his new role of daily commuter. Whether it's the nightly trips up to Connecticut to be with Ellen...or the Retirement-Date that he has circled on his calendar, they've given him a purpose outside of his job; to live his life and finally love again.

Chapter 78

The dawn breaks on Friday morning and Renee is awake with the crack of it. He continues shaving off the last three days of growth as Carolan approaches his cell door,

"Pssst...Renee. We need to talk man."

Renee finishes his grooming then walks over to the bars,

"What ya got?"

Carolan surveys the area to make sure the coast is clear,

"You told me to tell ya if something

was up with LeSean Jeffries...

well something's up."

Renee scratches his newly shaved chin, nods and gestures for him to continue,

"Seems that Jeffries is on a short list

of suspects for whacking your Grannie

and Cousin Philippe."

Renee's blood starts to boil,

"They've got a Detective coming

out here later to grill him."

Renee backs away from his cell door as madness erupts in his eyes. He

grits his teeth and begins to speak in tongues,

"Sorry if I fucked up Renee...

just thought that you'd

wanna know."

Noticing Renee's uncontrollable furor, Carolan quickly flees the area.

Renee paces like a wild animal in his cage,

"Your mine LeSean...up close and personal."

Slapping himself across the face to regain his composure,

"Get it together Renee...

got some planning to do."

Chapter 79

Detective Tim sits across the Prison's interrogation table from LeSean and his high-priced Attorney. LeSean has just finished a secret conversation with his lawyer when Tim barks out,

"I've got it straight from the

District Attorney's mouth.

Just cop to wasting Grannie

and Philippe Detaile' and the

death penalty will be off the

table."

LeSean's attorney, a tall Panamanian named Lee Mosquera, calmly adjusts his perfectly tailored suit-jacket then loudly responds,

"Scott...I am assuming that's Scott

Phillips is on the other end of your

Bluetooth, correct Detective?"

Unfazed and unresponsive to Lee's inquiry, Tim stays focused on LeSean,

"Scott, if you had anything concrete,

I wouldn't be here right now...

would I Mr. District Attorney?

Tim stares at LeSean as Scott says into his earpiece,

"Shit...Tell Lee I send my condolences for

picking up this case. And tell him we are

going to nail the door shut on his

asshole client."

Tim begins to tell Lee,

"Scott sends his condolences for picking..."

Lee interrupts Tim,

"I know, I know...you're gonna nail the

door shut...yada yada."

LeSean adds to the mix,

"That's right all you suit-wearing fucks...

you've got nothing on me...I've been

to the Detaile's hundreds of times,

but I was in Baltimore..."

Lee slams his fist on the table, but then calmly states,

"What my client *meant* to say is that

he's been to the Detaile' residence

in the past, but has no earthly-idea

as to what you may be implying.

He was clearly in Baltimore at that

time visiting the mother of his child."

"That's right you fuckin' pigs...

call my fuckin' ho if you wanna

check."

Lee stands then slides his chair dramatically away from the table,

"We're done here Mr. District Attorney.

My client will serve out the time he has

left on his previous conviction...

contact my office if you have anything

actually credible to discuss."

The attending C.O. removes LeSean's restraints, then Lee storms away

from the table with his client in-tow. Tim sits befuddled,

"What just happened Scott?"

"Don't worry. They've just won round

one,I was expecting that. This is a long

fight and we're in-it to win-it."

"Cool"

"I've got a plan in place...we're going to

use the media to our advantage for

a change."

Tim shakes his head yes,

"In-it to win-it...I'm totally down

with that."

"Excellent...we'll, let's get to

work then."

Tim exits the interrogation room as he continues talking with Scott.

Chapter 80

Settling into Dr. Alton's comfy red couch, Alexis and Ellen chat as they wait for his return from an emergency phone call,

"Ellen, I was so looking forward to our
session today. Sorry that I haven't
shared much. I've been kinda distracted
about what to do with my new job at
the prison."

"Don't worry about it, share a little or
a lot…whatever you're comfortable with."

-----Alexis replays Ellen's words, "share a little or a lot" in her head. Could she actually tell Ellen her true intentions at the prison? Reveal the only reason she donated the money was to exact her revenge? She thinks better of that notion and keeps it locked away for now-----

"It's just that once I got started serving
food to the inmates, this one guy scared
the hell out of me."

Dr. Alton walks in and hears the conversation,

"I did have my reservations Alexis…
about starting at the prison, but I'm

glad to see that you tried, but it just

wasn't your cup of tea."

"Yup. Plus seeing how well my girl

Ellen has pulled it all off...

coming back from her tragedy and

now she's even in love."

Alexis squeezes Ellen's hand,

"You're my inspiration Ellen...

your laughter, your openness."

She adoringly looks at Dr. Alton,

"And you Dr. Alton...I didn't think

it was possible to ever see beyond

tomorrow. Allowing me...no,

encouraging me to spill-out my guts

and put all those terrible emotions

on the table...you saved me from myself.

I will be eternally grateful to you both."

Dr. Alton scratches a few notes down in their file then calls for Mrs. Duvall

over the intercom,

"Can you come in here Mrs. D?"

From the other side of the intercom,

　　"I'll be right there."

Moments later, Mrs. Duvall walks in on Alexis and Ellen embracing and she smiles ear-to-ear,

　　"This wonderful Healing Room...

　　it always finds a way to work magic."

Dr. Alton cheers,

　　"Here Here...I concur completely."

Mrs. D. asks everyone,

　　"Who needs something to drink?"

After the girls release their embrace, Alexis sniffles an answer,

　　"I'd love a soda...think I'm dehydrated

　　from all the waterworks."

Ellen wipes her eyes,

　　"Me too Mrs. D...thanks."

Dr. Alton waves his finger in a circle above his head,

　　"Then Cola's for everyone...

　　we've done some serious work

　　here tonight ladies."

Mrs. Duvall quickly goes to the refrigerator in the corner of the room, retrieves four cans of soda and brings them over on a tray. Dr. Alton speaks in a very serious tone,

> "This, being our last court-ordered
>
> session, has drawn to a close the
>
> mandatory portion of our relationship
>
> ladies…and you both appear to be in
>
> a much better place."

Ellen and Alexis nod their heads in agreement,

> "But I do believe that we've only
>
> scratched the surface."

The girls look at each other and in unison,

> "Every Friday at five Dr. Alton."

Alexis adds,

> "You're not getting rid of us
>
> that easy Doc."

He smiles then says to Mrs. D,

> "Well then…every Friday at five it is…
>
> can you pencil that in my
>
> schedule Mrs. D?"

Playfully grabbing the girls by their cheeks,

"I already have Jeffrey. I just knew

these two girls were gonna gel."

They all pop open their sodas then cheer,

"To the Healing Room."

Chapter 81

While driving up to Connecticut Saturday morning, Scott calls

Derrick over his cell phone,

"Bossman...what's up?"

Scott checks the traffic in his rearview mirror,

"On my way to pick-up Ellen...

didn't have a chance to call you

until just now. Turn on the

Channel 7 News buddy...

my plan's already in motion."

Derrick grabs the T.V. remote and switches to the appropriate station. The

"Channel 7 Breaking News" banner is plastered on the bottom of the

screen as a reporter announces,

"Stuart Doland, live and on the scene

here for Channel 7 News with an

exclusive report."

The recent video of a Corrections Officer being led away in handcuffs is

shown on the television,

"Shown here being taken into custody

is Mark Carolan, a corrections officer

who's been indicted for the recent

video-hacking of the Prison's

security system. He's also being

investigated for his involvement

in the recent deadly explosion

at the prison."

A photo of LeSean flashes on-screen as the reporter continues,

"From a high-ranking official at the

District Attorney's office, this reporter

has learned that LeSean Jeffries has

been linked to Officer Carolan and

is the lead suspect in the brutal slaying

of five this past Christmas Eve."

The reporter comes back on-screen and speaks into his microphone,

"There's been a $150,000 reward issued

for any information leading to the

conviction of this dangerous suspect,

who is due to be released from prison

within the month."

Derrick turns off the television and belts-out,

"You ARE the man Scott."

Derrick laughs,

      "A high ranking official at the District

      Attorney's office...I love it."

Scott looks at himself in the rearview mirror and strokes his hair,

      "Just like you said buddy...

      Go big or go home."

Chapter 82

As she cracks her eyes open to welcome in a new day, Alexis is filled with a strange feeling of peace and serenity. The horrible stench of rotting flesh has finally lifted from her mind. The blooming of a jasmine plant, just outside of her open window, wafts an aroma that refreshes her senses,

"Sweet...a weekend to do

whatever I want."

After swiping some butter on her toast, Alexis takes a seat at her kitchen table and turns on the counter-top television. Scanning for something watchable, the Channel 7 News Bulletin catches her notice,

"LeSean Jeffries, pictured here, is believed

to be connected with the Christmas Eve

slaying of five..."

LeSean's mugshot appearing on the T.V. screen is all it took.

Alexis calmly rises from her seat and turns off the television. Walking in a trance over to her fridge, Alexis swings open the door then grabs a package from the bottom shelf. After tearing open the postage, she reaches into it then pulls out a small vile marked "Thallium Nitrate". Holding it up to her eyes,

"Damn...the internet is such a

wonderful thing."

She taps the small bottle with her fingernail,

"LeSean Jeffries...welcome to

MY nightmare."

Alexis grabs her Prison I.D. Badge hanging on a lanyard near the fridge.

After heading up to her bedroom to change clothes, she then sets-off to

grab a volunteering shift at the Prison. The time has finally come for Alexis

to fully embrace her and LeSean's twisted-destiny.

Chapter 83

Since the arrest of Carolan earlier this morning, the prison's been on lockdown. As two Correction's Officers stand guard near Renee's cage, he calls out to them,

"What's happening fellas? Carolan took

the easy-way out I heard...hung himself

with his shoelaces. Damn shame...

somebody musta had some serious

shit on Carolan, for him to go off

himself like that."

Laughing loudly, Renee recalls the last encounter in his cell with Carolan...

"...Listen Carolan...shit's gonna

get real...real fuckin' soon."

Sweating bullets, Carolan begs Renee for help,

"Please Renee...don't hurt them...

they're all I got in the world."

After brutally smacking Carolan across the mouth, Renee continues,

"Well then...as I see it, you've only

got one choice. Be a fuckin' man and

do it...you know me Carolan, I am a

man of my mother fuckin' word."

Carolan shakes his head yes, reluctantly agreeing to Renee's demand,

"And just remember...you were a

dead man anyway. This way, you're

assured the Carolan family name

will be carried on by your son."

...With Renee still laughing aloud, one of the guarding C.O.'s can't contain

his composure any longer.

Smashing his baton across Renee's cell bars,

"You fuckin' scumbag...

I'm gonna kill you..."

"Go easy Hatcher" barks the

second Officer, "He aint fuckin'

worth it."

Hatcher eases-up as Renee further taunts them,

"That's right man...go easy. You never

know who...or what's waitin' round

the next corner for ya."

Renee sits back in his cot and reassesses the new situation. The lockdown

has put a crimp into his plans for wasting LeSean,

"Twenty -three hours of lockdown...

only three open meal sessions

with the rest of the bloc's general

population. How the fuck am I

gonna make this happen?

Gotta hit LeSean like a ton of bricks...

but will I even get the chance before

he's outta my grasp for good?"

Renee strokes his weathered chin and recalculates his dwindling options.

Chapter 84

An hour or so after his arrival, Scott sits on the porch of the Connecticut house enjoying a fine Cuban cigar. He slowly exhales as Ellen calls out his name from inside the house,

"Scott...come in here quick babe."

Scott places the Cohiba down in the crystal ashtray then darts inside through the sliding glass doorway,

"What's up doll face, where's the fire?"

Ellen presses the speaker button on her cellphone, then Dr. Paul's voice calls-out,

"Hey there guys...got some great

news for you. I think I've found

your Chelsea."

Ellen kisses Scott then screeches out,

"What? I can't believe it...

I love you Dr. Paul. How did

you find her?"

"Once I broadened the search for her...

I knew that it was only a matter of time

before we had a hit...her name is

Chelsea Charles and her case fits

all the parameters."

Scott squeezes Ellen tightly then asks,

"So where is she Paul?"

"Up in Brockton, Massachusetts...

at Good Samaritan Hospital.

There's some kind of patient-privacy

issues with Chelsea...I couldn't find

any next-of-kin for her and the hospital's

thrown up a brick wall at me."

Ellen nervously asks Scott,

"So what do we do baby?

How are we gonna find out

what's going on?"

Scott scratches his chin then determines their best course of action,

"Paul...I need you to jump on a

plane and meet us up in Massachusetts.

Ellen smiles as Scott continues,

"Sophia's on her way up to Connecticut

already...we'll wait for her, then we'll

drive up and meet you at the hospital...

okay buddy?"

"For you Big Guy, the world...Dr. Paul out."

Ellen runs to Scott and throws her arms around him. She pecks him five or

six times quickly on his cheek,

"Sophia's gonna be here anytime...

I need to get ready. I'm sooooo excited."

Ellen bolts towards the master bedroom and readies for their trek to

Massachusetts.

Chapter 85

Alexis casually walks through the prison's metal-detector then flashes her I.D. to the attending Corrections Officer. Checking his electronic-schedule, the C.O. indicates for Alexis to halt,

"We don't have you scheduled for

today's shift Ms. Weinstein.

Are you here to meet with someone?"

Alexis thinks to herself,

"You're damn right I'm here to meet

someone...I'm gonna kill LeSean Jeffries

and who gives a shit of the consequences...

I'm gonna be dead in six months anyway."

Alexis sweetly answers him,

"Just call Dr. Gayle Andrews honey...

I've got an open-ended volunteer

status here."

The C.O. quickly dials, waits for a response and after explaining the current situation to Dr. Gayle, he waves Alexis by,

"Dr. Gayle sends her regards...

please have a great day."

She cordially nods, makes her way through the prison's last checkpoint then adjusts the vial of poison nestled into her bra. With a confidant stride, Alexis makes her way through the corridors then onward to the prison's cafeteria.

STEP ONE...Complete

Scott motors his BMW 7 Series up the highway to Brockton. Ellen and Sophia are sprawled-out in the spacious back seat,

"I'm so glad you're here Sophia...

there's no way I'm keeping it

together without you."

Sophia opens the back window a crack,

"Where else would I be sweetie?

Of course, with my best friend

on her way up to finally figure out

her little Tommy's puzzle."

Sophia finishes a sip of her bottled water then asks Scott,

"So what's the latest from Dr. Paul?"

After changing lanes on the highway, Scott answers,

"The latest info is that Chelsea had a

traumatic accident the day after Christmas...

she's been at Good Samaritan Hospital

ever since. Paul's working on every angle

for us, but we really just got to get up

there and make this happen."

Glancing down, Scott notices on the car's display that Derrick's calling. He taps the ANSWER icon then Derrick's voice comes over the car's speakers.

"Hey everybody...Paul tells me that

you're on the way up to Mass."

Sophia calls out,

"You got that right Detective Handsome...

how ya feel in' darlin'?"

"Feeling great gorgeous, thanks."

With concern, Scott interjects,

"We're running into some static

with the hospital up there...any help..."

"Don't worry, I've dropped a line to a

buddy of mine up there in Brockton...

Detective Colombo. They're a big family

up in those parts...lotta influence.

He should be able help you guys out."

With added encouragement, Scott pounds on the steering wheel,

"Thanks Derrick...you never stop plugging

for me old friend."

"I asked Guy to meet you guys at the hospital.

Just text me when you get there, then I'll send

him right over to me ya."

The girls hug each other as Derrick responds,

"Just get up there safe...

I've got this sponge-bath date with a

beautiful nurse to get ready for."

Ellen calls to Derrick lovingly,

"Thank you so much Derrick...

for everything!"

Scott mashes on the accelerator pedal and they bolt up the highway...and on to Good Samaritan Hospital.

Chapter 87

A seemingly endless line of convicts, all waiting for their afternoon chow, slows Alexis' time perception to a snail's pace. The deadly vial is concealed perfectly up her sleeve...like a trap, ready to be sprung, she serves them their mashed potatoes.

As face after face passes by, Alexis' heart begins to throb in her throat...the anticipation of her end-game is palpable,

"It won't be long...

the food line's almost up."

Alexis glances down the row, but no LeSean to be seen,

"Where can he be? Did I somehow

subconsciously miss him on purpose?"

She finishes serving the final inmate,

"Something had to have happened...

get it together Alexis...just gotta be

laser focused for tonight's dinner.

He's gotta be here."

Checking to make sure that no one's watching her, Alexis slides the vial back into her bra,

"That's right...Ellen did mention that

the Detective Tim was going to meet

with a suspect in the case...that's just

gotta be it. Bide your time Alexis...

it'll happen."

-----At the very same moment, LeSean is just finishing-up his meeting with

Lee Mosquera.

"Just keep your nose clean for the rest

of the month LeSean...you'll be flying

free as a bird. Ready to create some

new mayhem somewhere, I'm sure."

LeSean reaches over the Conference Room table and shakes Lee's hand

vigorously,

"Now that's funny...you do know me

Mosquera, don't ya. I know that you

know my money really well too,

don't ya Lee?"

Lee stands, walks towards the conference room door but quickly turns,

"Keep it under control Jeffries...

let's never have to see each other

again, okay? I don't care for your

company and would rather never

see your face again."

Lee raps on the heavy door then it swings open. As he exits LeSean laughs

aloud,

"Thanks for the advice Lee...

and the get outta jail free card.

Worth every fuckin' penny!"

Chapter 88

Ellen and Sophia patiently wait for Scott to finish his conversation with the Hospital Administrator from Good Samaritan. He gestures over, with a wave, to follow him and the Administrator down the hall. Once they reach him, Ellen grabs hold of Scott's hand,

"What's going on babe?"

Shrugging his shoulders,

"The Administrator is going to explain

what's happening in just a minute...

we need to follow him to his office first."

Ellen exhales deeply, with disappointment. Sophia then comes up from

behind and places her hand on her shoulder,

"Hang in there sweetie...

we've already come this far."

Nodding her head in understanding,

"I know, I'm just dying to meet Chelsea.

I have so many questions for her."

Scott places his massive arms around Ellen and Sophia as they follow the

administrator to his office.

"Come on girls...we're almost home."

After reaching the office, they all take their seats,

"District Attorney Phillips...we want to

help you, but the extenuating

circumstances relating to Chelsea's

case has our hands tied. What I can

tell you is that Ms. Charles did sustain

life-threatening injuries in a car

accident and has been treated here

ever since. She had a DNR request

attached to her driver's license,

but the EMT thought her condition

at the time superseded any

previous request."

Sophia quickly barks,

"Her condition...what the hell

does that mean?"

The Administrator, annoyed with Sophia's outburst, stands and quickly

heads towards his door. But just before exiting, he defiantly states,

"I'm sorry about your situation, but

hospital policy prohibits me from

having any further conversation

about the subject. Good day and

please show yourselves out."

He disappears down the corridor as they all sit dumbfounded. Rising

slowly from their chairs, Sophia whimsically says,

> "Tommy sure would be proud of
>
> this riddle he spawned...
>
> right up his alley."

Ellen agrees,

> "Unbelievable. Why can't I just
>
> see her?"

While reassuringly stroking Ellen's shoulder, Scott reminds her,

> "Let's not give-up hope. Dr. Paul is
>
> on his way and he'll definitely help out.
>
> Trust me...we're not budging until I
>
> get some answers."

Adding to his sentiment, Sophia tries to make-up for her faux pas with the

Administrator,

> "And remember, Derrick is sending his
>
> buddy too. I texted him when we first
>
> got here so it's only a matter of time."

They exit the Administrator's office and head back towards the hospital's waiting area.

Chapter 89

As she mops the prison's kitchen floor, Alexis fantasizes about LeSean enduring the debilitating cramps associated with Thallium Nitrate poisoning. The vivid image of his wide-eyed death-gaze, as he struggles for life, settles deep into her psyche...and it warms her,

"Just one more hour then it's

game-time" she mutters to herself

while ringing-out a mop.

Throwing the newly readied swab to the floor, Alexis begins to vigorously clean,

"Let's get this place spic-n-span...

then I'll get rid of the rest of the

dirt with one fell swoop."

Another Volunteer passes closely by and hears Alexis talking to herself,

"You okay honey? Not answering your

own questions, I hope."

Alexis comes outta her fog,

"I'm Sorry...what?"

The Volunteer playfully remarks,

"I thought I heard you talking

to yourself..."

Rapidly checking the name on Alexis' ID badge,

"...Alexis."

Alexis coyly shrugs her shoulders,

"No...I just really get into cleaning."

The Volunteer scans the newly cleaned floor,

"I can see that, what a great job...

this place looks immaculate."

"Why thank you...we aims to please."

As the Volunteer wave's goodbye, Alexis glances at the clock hanging

upon the wall...time for Step Two.

"Here we go Alexis...

all or nothing."

Chapter 90

While Scott is across the room retrieving coffee for Ellen and

Sophia, Dr. Paul and a very tall man approach them at a rapid pace. Paul

waves over at Scott then warmly says to the girls,

"Sophia, Ellen...let me introduce an old

buddy of mine and Derrick's...

Detective Guy Colombo."

The Detective reaches out and shakes both their hands as Scott reaches

the group,

"Paul, how ya doing?

This must be Detective Colombo."

They shake hands as Guy responds,

"It's a pleasure. Now from what Paul

and Derrick tell me, you got some

wicked problems getting any

information...right?"

They all nod and Guy continues,

"Well lucky for you all, I'm known as

the Information Man. I've already left a

message for my great-uncle, Dr. Joe Colombo,

He just *happens* to sit on the Board of this

esteemed hospital and I can..."

Without hesitation Ellen runs up to Guy and hugs him. She pulls away and

whispers to him,

"All I need Detective...is to just meet

with Chelsea. I need to say hello and

thank her for bringing joy into my

Tommy's world."

The usually brash and crusty Detective is moved by Ellen's sentiment,

"Consider it already done my dear."

Guy pulls a cellphone from his pocket and gets to making it happen for

this newly found friends,

"Hi, Dr. DePasqua, it's Colombo

here...is my Uncle Joe available?"

Struggling to hide her excitement, Ellen leaps into Scott's arms,

"I feel it babe...Detective Columbo is

going to come through for us...

I just know it."

"I think you're right doll."

Sophia chimes-in,

"I'm crossing my fingers and toes

for ya sweetie."

Chapter 91

The prison's dinner-bell rings out, calling the inmates to take their positions on the food line. Alexis readies herself at the meatloaf station with her deadly ampoule tucked away...she's ready to strike.

There's no heart-pounding this time...no rush of adrenaline as Alexis spots LeSean at the end of the serving line, with tray in hand. Just a steady calm as he gradually makes his way closer,

"Here it is Alexis" she thinks to

herself as she slides the poison

into place.

"As easy as buttering your morning

Toast Alexis."

LeSean reaches-out his food tray...but then dramatically pulls it back from her station,

"Wait a minute...

I remember that face now..."

...LeSean flashes back to Christmas Eve. Alexis' face, on so many photos hanging around the Weinstein's house, comes rushing back to him...

"...you're that bitch I saw that night...

in all the pictures hanging round that

Jew couple's house."

He leans closer to her and in a soft voice,

"You shoulda heard your mom scream

when I cut her fuckin' finger off.

I'm outta here in a month bitch

then I'm gonna come to visit you."

Just as LeSean begins to devilishly smile and laugh aloud,

"You Bastard!" gasps a Corrections

Officer from five feet away of LeSean.

The wounded C.O. crumples to the floor as Renee runs past him. He

quickly grabs LeSean from behind and plunges a four-inch shank into

Jeffries' right kidney. He follows that plunge with an abrupt upstroke,

causing blood to spew from LeSean's mouth...and it splatters across

Alexis' face.

Renee continues the assault...He rips the makeshift blade from

LeSean's back then begins to slice his throat from ear-to ear. Slowly

whispering to LeSean as the life runs out of his body,

"Payback for Grannie and the boys

Jeffries...have a nice trip to hell."

Tossing LeSean to the floor,

"And I'll see you there soon."

LeSean's pumping neck wound splashes the cafeteria floor with blood as Renee slowly drops to his knees. Placing his hands behind his head, Renee allows the onrushing Officers to tackle him to the floor without any resistance,

"I'm all yours boys...definitely worth it."

Amongst all the chaos, Alexis calmly pours her deadly concoction down the sink's drain. First rinsing the vial, she then washes her face clean of all the remnants of LeSean's essence,

"STEP TWO...Complete, and without

having to lift a finger."

She removes the blood-stained apron and drops it to the floor. Alexis then walks towards her escape from all of this madness for good. A beautiful smile appears on her face as a revelation comes to her mind,

"STEP THREE...Go kick Cancer's Ass."

Chapter 92

Ellen and Scott slowly enter Chelsea's hospital room, not sure of exactly what to expect. Attending to Chelsea is a nurse who's quietly notating the results of a monitor's data. Taking notice of them entering the room,

"Praise the Lord...finally some family
to come and see Chelsea. I've been
hoping that someone would come
and visit."

"Yes...we are her family...Chelsea was
engaged to my Tommy. I've been
waiting to meet her."

The nurse waves Ellen closer,

"Well, c'mon over here dear...
don't be afraid. I'm gonna jump
out of your way and let you two
get acquainted."

Ellen looks at Scott for reassurance. He gently nudges her,

"Go ahead baby...I'll be right outside...
you two need some time alone."

Ellen kisses him then walks over to Chelsea's bedside. The nurse whispers

to Scott as he holds the door open for them to exit,

>"I'm going to let Dr. Turner know
>
>that you're here. I'm positive he'd
>
>want to meet you both."

As the door swings shut, Scott has an aha-moment,

>"Dr. Turner...oh my God."

Scott pulls-out his wallet and shows the nurse his identification,

>"I'm District Attorney Scott Phillips...
>
>will you please take me to see
>
>Dr. Turner?"
>
>"Certainly Mr. District Attorney...
>
>follow me, I'll take you right to him."

He trails her down the hall, on a mission to meet the ever-elusive Dr.

Turner.

Chapter 93

Ellen gently strokes the only spot on Chelsea's arm that doesn't have a tube sticking out of it,

"Oh, why my dear Chelsea...why couldn't

we have met under different circumstances?

Why here...and why now? They told me

you're never waking-up. Oh, how I pray

that you know that you're loved Chelsea...

and that you're not alone."

She drops her face into her hands and begins to cry,

"I hope that you can hear me...

I'm here for you Chelsea."

Just then, Sophia enters the room and rushes to Ellen's side,

"Oh darlin'...please don't cry. At least

we know who she is now...

and you can be here for her."

Ellen continues sobbing as Sophia drapes her arms around her,

"But Sophia...now I'll never know.

No answers to all those questions

that are haunting me."

She puts her hands on each of Ellen's shoulders then wipes away her

tears,

> "Let's go find Scott and get you home...
>
> it's been a long day."

Reluctantly Ellen agrees,

> "Sounds like a plan Sophia.
>
> I'll come back soon to stay with her."

Ellen stands, leans over Chelsea's bed and kisses her upon the forehead.

Sophia gently urges,

> "C'mon sweetie...let's go for now."

Ellen's IPhone vibrates...it's an incoming text from Scott. She taps on the

IPhone's screen then reads his message,

> "Please come to the ICU waiting room...
>
> I have two people that I'm dying for
>
> you to meet. Love you babe!!"

Ellen sighs and tells Sophia,

> "I don't think I'm up to meeting
>
> anyone right now...what's he thinking?"

> "I trust the Big Guy's instincts sweetie.
>
> Let's head over and see what he's

talking about."

Ellen texts back an "ok" as they leave Chelsea's room.

Chapter 94

Sophia grabs the handle of the ICU waiting room door and opens it. Slinking into the room, Ellen is greeted by a broadly smiling, open-armed Scott as Paul and Detective Colombo vociferously call out her name,

"Ellen...we're so happy for you!"

A completely confused Ellen turns to Sophia,

"What's going on here?"

Sophia shrugs her shoulders,

"I have no earthly idea."

Scott rushes over, picks Ellen up off her feet and hugs her tightly. Like a big bear, he carries her effortlessly to meet the first of her mystery dates,

"Let me first introduce you to

Dr. Turner honey...THE Dr. Turner...

the one you've been searching for."

The gray-haired doctor reaches out and shakes her hand,

"Pleasure's all mine Ms. Carpenter."

A thoroughly confused Ellen questions the doctor,

"Dr. Turner...what are you doing in

a people's hospital? I don't understand."

Dr. Turner calmly explains,

> "First of all Ellen, I'm not a veterinarian...
>
> I'm on-staff here at Good Samaritan Hospital.
>
> Chelsea and little Thomas were already
>
> patients of mine before their horrible tragedy."

Ellen shakes her head in surprise,

> "Chelsea and Thomas were your patients?
>
> Now you totally lost me doc."

Dr. Turner reaches into his pocket, pulls out a small slip of paper and shows it to Ellen,

> "This is what the EMT found in
>
> Chelsea's hand...when he attended
>
> to her injuries at the crash scene.
>
> They resuscitated her there and
>
> she's been on life-support ever since."

Ellen begins to read Chelsea's note,

> Mommy--Chelsea Charles
>
> Daddy----Thomas Carpenter
>
> Spud------Thomas Charles Carpenter

Dr. Turner informs Ellen that Chelsea didn't have any relatives,

"You are now Chelsea's next of kin."

"I'm Chelsea's what?"

"Next of kin. She had no other-living

relatives...until last week. We tried to

find the right Thomas Carpenter

but there were literally thousands

to choose from."

Ellen's eyes rise from the note. She catches sight of a Nurse carrying a

swaddled baby through a doorway. Scott reaches over and grabs Ellen by

the hand,

"Dr. Turner is Chelsea's

OB/GYN honey...the other fella

I wanted you to meet is right here."

The nurse hands Ellen an "angel dropped from heaven",

"Meet your grandson sweetheart...

this is Thomas Charles Carpenter."

A million emotions pour through Ellen's mind as she gazes down at little

Tommy...and at that very moment, she finds her new unconditional love.

The room erupts with complete revelry as Sophia rushes over,

kisses Ellen on the cheek then pecks Little Tommy upon his forehead. The guys are sharing a long group hug when Ellen tugs at Scott's shirt sleeve.

Breaking away from the merriment,

> "Yeah babe?"

While carefully holding her new-life's joy, Ellen kisses Scott,

> "I'm so tired...let's get Little Tommy
>
> home as soon as possible."

After kissing Scott again,

> "But please...make sure that we take
>
> care of everything with Chelsea first...
>
> okay babe?"

He adjusts the baby's blanket with one hand while tenderly touching her cheek with the other,

> "Sure babe....I'm on it."

Scott swings his arm around Ellen then kisses the top of her head. They begin to write their new story together...as a family.

Epilogue

Now halfway through his terrible-two's, little Tommy, or TJ as he implores to be called, is playing

with Scott in the backyard of the Connecticut house.

The full brunt of a north-east December has blanketed the area in white as Scott places the head on TJ's first snowman. From about fifty feet away in her second-floor art studio, Ellen intently watches her two boys frolic in the snow. After one last glance, Ellen turns to her canvass and applies a brush stroke. Smiling with accomplishment, she recognizes that she hasn't lost that artisan's flair.

After placing down her brush, Ellen walks to the window and waves down to Scott. He blows her a kiss then effortlessly lifts TJ, high enough to place the carrot for Frosty's nose...throwing her back to the memory of her and Big Tommy's first snowman. Lightly touching the chilled windowpanes, and in happy wonderment, Ellen thinks of how far she's come since losing Tommy.

Returning to her easel, she spots Alexis and Michael's wedding photo hanging on her wall,

"That's right Alexis...all those patient

years of waiting and you finally found

your Mr. Right."

She chuckles remembering the story of how the couple had met,

"Your second-cousin saved the

day again, huh? How that horrible

prom story morphed into meeting

your Cousin Paul's best friend Michael."

Ellen slips off into a sweet memory of Alexis and Michael's wedding day...

...Sophia and Ellen are adjusting Alexis's dress and veil. Sophia

steps back to survey their handiwork,

"You look just like an angel Alexis."

Ellen adjusts a final curl of Alexis' hair,

"Just like a fairy princess."

Alexis looks at her reflection in the full-length mirror, smiles then turns to

the girls,

"I can't believe MY day is finally here...

I've wished for someone like

Michael my whole life."

She again scans her reflection,

"And I am breathtaking Daddy...

you were right."

The three share an embrace.

...Ellen's face saddens recalling Alexis and Michael's last kiss... With Ellen and Sophia draped at her feet, Alexis whispers the words "I love you" to Michael. He gently presses his lips to hers and after sharing that last kiss, she succumbs to her cancer.

...Ellen's recollections are broken by the sounds of Scott and TJ rustling up the stairwell to the second floor. Moments later, TJ comes rushing through her door,

"Gigi" TJ calls out as he darts

towards her.

Scooping him up into her arms, she hugs him at length,

"Oh...Gigi loves you so much

little man."

While sharing their embrace, Scott walks over and kisses her upon the nose. TJ points at the area of her art studio that's been set up as his playroom,

"Train Gigi...TJ wants train."

She walks over to the play area, places TJ down as Scott stares intensely at her painting,

"Wow babe...this is awesome."

He notices a small green spot in the left corner of the canvas hidden in the

wintry scene. After bending down and squinting to get a better look,

"What are these little flowers in

the corner of your painting babe?

They look like dandelions."

She rushes over to him and rewards his insight with a big kiss,

"Exactly right my perceptive man...

my Daddy used to call me his

Buttercup Dandelion...because

when I was twelve, I was nothing

but long legs and blonde hair."

She points at the flowers,

"If you look real close, you'll see

that one of the dandelion heads

have popped-off."

She kisses him again,

"You and TJ have made me so

happy sweetie."

Breaking their tender moment, Sophia enters the room,

"Oops...sorry guys."

Scott pecks Ellen one last time,

"No problem...what's up Ms. Miller?"

Sophia flips through a legal pad emboldened with the name,

Phillips and Associates===Attorney

at Law/Detective Agency"

After Scott retired last year, so many people kept asking for legal

advice...it was a no-brainer to hire Sophia full-time and get Phillips and

Associates up and running. Sophia finds her place in the notepad,

"I just got off the phone with

Derrick and Detective Bowdish.

The two professors who were

abducted from Princeton and

Harvard last week...they've tied it

to something that's gonna hit

home Scott."

Scott leans back on the wall,

"What's going on Sophia?"

"It hasn't been reported in the

news yet, but your old friend

Dr. Anderson from Yale was taken

at gunpoint early this morning.

The boys are confident all three

kidnappings are related."

Ellen notices that Scott and Sophia have shifted back into attack-mode,

"Alright you two...go get to work

and let me get some painting done...

okay?"

Scott winks at her,

"You got it babe. Okay Sophia,

let's get your newly-renovated

office into action. I'll need the

Governor's offices of New Jersey,

Mass and Connecticut in the bullpen

so we can coordinate our actions."

Giving him a thumbs-up,

"I'm on it boss...right away."

Scott grabs his phone and readies for the action.

An hour or so later, Sophia transfers a call to Scott's phone,

"Got Governor Paulson on line 2 Scott."

"Perfect...thanks doll."

Turning to her computer, she contemplates what to input for Case #1.

She's got it..!

"Case #1...Abductions at the Ivy Covered Walls."

THE END

Made in the USA
Middletown, DE
31 July 2019